"I _____ This Baby In The Middle Of Highway 81,"

Maddie said to the stranger, panic racing through her. "Listen, I'll cook you dinner for a year if you'll just take me to the hospital on your motorcycle—"

Another contraction hit. By the time the pain passed, the man was carefully placing a helmet on her head.

"Thank you so very much," she said, fighting tears of relief.

"Save your thank-yous for when you get to the hospital," he muttered before he mounted the bike.

Maddie shot the motorcycle a doubtful look and gingerly straddled it.

"Are you on?"

"Yes," she whispered.

"All I want you to do is hold on. I'm gonna move as quickly and easily as I can. When you feel a contraction coming on, squeeze me, yell at me, kick me—just let me know."

Her opinion of him rose ten feet. He was strong. He was practical.

Most important, he was there.

Dear Reader,

There's something for everyone this month! Brides, babies and cowboys...but also humor, sensuality...and delicious love stories (some without a baby in sight!).

There's nothing as wonderful as a new book from Barbara Boswell, and this month we have a MAN OF THE MONTH written by this talented author. *Who's the Boss?* is a very sexy, delightfully funny love story. As always, Barbara not only creates a masterful hero and smart-as-a-whip heroine, she also makes her secondary characters come alive!

When a pregnant woman gets stuck in a traffic jam she does the only thing she can do—talks a handsome hunk into giving her a ride to the hospital on his motorcycle in Leanne Banks's latest, *The Troublemaker Bride*.

Have you ever wanted to marry a millionaire? Well, heroine Irish Ellison plans on finding a man with money in *One Ticket to Texas* by Jan Hudson. A single mom-to-be gets a new life in Paula Detmer Riggs's emotional and heartwarming *Daddy by Accident*. And a woman with a "bad reputation" finds unexpected romance in Barbara McMahon's *Boss Lady and the Hired Hand*.

Going to your high-school reunion is bad enough. But what if you were voted "Most likely to succeed"...but your success at love has been fleeting? Well, that's just what happens in Susan Connell's *How To Succeed at Love*.

So read...and enjoy!

Lucia Macro

Lucia Macro
Senior Editor

LEANNE BANKS
THE TROUBLEMAKER BRIDE

SILHOUETTE *Desire*®
Published by Silhouette Books
America's Publisher of Contemporary Romance

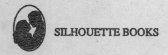 SILHOUETTE BOOKS

ISBN 0-373-76070-1

THE TROUBLEMAKER BRIDE

Printed in U.S.A.

LEANNE BANKS

is a national number-one bestselling author of romance. Recognized for her sensual writing with a Career Achievement Award from *Romantic Times* magazine, Leanne likes creating a story with a few grins, a generous kick of sensuality and characters that hang around after the book is finished.

The "How To Catch a Princess" trilogy was inspired by Leanne's memories of her childhood and is set in Roanoke, Virgina, where Leanne grew up. Leanne loves to hear from readers. You can write to her at P.O. Box 1442, Midlothian, VA 23113.

Special acknowledgments to Margaret, Debbie and Debra for all the fun we had strumming our badminton rackets for our Monkees band practice.

Prologue

Nine-year-old Maddie Palmer dropped the needle on the record and made a quick dash for the bar stool. She scrambled onto the seat and stood. "One, two, three, four!" she yelled out just like Davey Rogers of the Pink Bubblegum rock band.

Grinning at her pals, Emily and Jenna Jean, she belted out the opening chorus along with her favorite rock star. Her friends stood on top of the seats of matching brown vinyl bar stools and sang along. Since it was raining on Cherry Lane today, Maddie had talked the baby-sitter into letting her and her friends play in the basement.

Life was good. The baby-sitter let her play the music as loudly as she wanted. She'd just bought the new 45 record spinning on her record player. She was strumming her pretend guitar, a badminton racket, with her two best friends. Maddie was even wearing Emily's fancy tiara. And for once she wasn't grounded.

When the record ended with a loud static sound, Maddie jumped off the stool and ran to the record player. "Let's do it again," she said, holding the tiara in place with her other hand. "If we get good enough, maybe we could put on a show and charge people a quarter to hear us sing."

Dressed in a pink pinafore, Emily looked at her badminton racket doubtfully. "I don't know, Maddie. I don't think I'm a very good rock star."

Jenna Jean bounced her racket against her fist. "I don't know if anyone is gonna pay to see us. We might have to give them food or something. Those creepy boys would just laugh." She looked at Maddie. "Besides, these rackets look more like banjos than electric guitars."

"Well, maybe we could serve fruit punch and cookies," Maddie suggested, ignoring the comment about the badminton rackets since she couldn't do anything about it. She was more worried about her voice. She lived in mortal fear that her singing sounded as bad to others as it did to her, but she was too chicken to ask her friends to tell the truth, so she just sang as loudly as she could.

"Do you really want to be a rock star when you grow up? My mother says they hardly ever take a bath," Emily said with a shudder.

"Davey Rogers of the Pink Bubblegum rock band takes a bath," Maddie insisted. "I know cause I'm an official member of his fan club." Emily was a little bit prissy, but Maddie liked her because she was nice and shared her tiara. "I don't really have to be a rock star. I just want to be rich and go exciting places. I want to have adventures," she told her, then remembered her deepest wish of all. "And never get grounded again."

"I would go crazy if my mom made me stay in my yard as much as yours does," Jenna Jean said, swiveling her bar stool around as she stood on it. "It seems like you're always getting into trouble."

Maddie got a yucky feeling in the pit of her stomach. Sometimes she wondered what was wrong with her. Neither of her friends got grounded as often as she did. "I don't do anything that terrible."

She watched Jenna Jean swivel the chair again and thought about asking her to stop. Jenna Jean was a show-off, and Maddie's mother didn't like it when they stood on the bar stools.

"Nope," Jenna Jean said. "You know what your problem is."

"What?"

"You get caught."

The yucky feeling in her stomach got worse. Jenna Jean was a whole year older, and she was very smart. She even got As in Math. Maddie got Cs.

"Maybe," she admitted. "Maybe I'm just bad." Maddie didn't like to think about how often she got grounded. Hands on her hips, she turned to her friends. "Come on. While my mom's gone, let's practice this song again and pretend we're singing at the coliseum downtown."

She dropped the needle on the record and scrambled on top of the chair again. Her hands poised to strum the badminton racket, her mouth open and ready to sing, she watched her mother enter the basement.

Maddie froze in horror.

Out of the corner of her eye, she saw Jenna Jean and Emily scramble off their stools, but Maddie couldn't seem to move her feet as her mother took in the scene with a disapproving expression.

"Young lady," her mother said, and Maddie sighed. Whenever her mother called her young lady, she was grounded.

"What are you doing standing on that bar stool? I've told you a dozen times not to stand on the bar stools. What if you or your friends got hurt?" She shook her finger at Maddie. "You've had your warning, now…"

Maddie glanced at Jenna Jean as her mother went on with her lecture. *Caught* again.

One

Maddie stared outside her car window. The same sight greeted her from all sides. Cars. Stopped cars.

She was in the middle of a traffic jam on Highway 81.

Caught again.

This sort of thing didn't happen in Roanoke, Virginia. The population wasn't dense enough to create a traffic problem, especially not on the highway. According to the radio, however, a sinkhole had given way smack dab in the middle lane, causing expected delays of up to two hours.

It might have been okay if she were in the right-hand lane and could use the curb to reach her destination, but she was in the middle lane. It wasn't as if she was in a rush to get to her job as a travel agent. She had taken the day off. It wasn't as if she had a pressing dinner date either. She hadn't been on a dinner date in about nine months.

Her problem was the rhythmic tightening of the muscles in her back and abdomen, slowly building, then peaking. More discomfort than pain, the tightening occurred every five minutes. Maddie kept telling herself the feeling would go away, but she suspected she was in labor. In the middle of the only traffic jam in the history of Roanoke, Virginia. In the rain. With no car phone.

Her stomach growled, and she wished for the fortieth time that she'd brought some cookies in the car with her. Another contraction hit, this one requiring the use of a breathing technique. Maddie visualized Maui, beautiful water, palm trees, rainbows. If she were in Maui, she would be sipping a Mai Tai. God knows, she could use something with liquor in it right now.

A thread of panic raced through her. She really didn't want to have her baby in the middle of a highway. Turning on her windshield wipers, she searched desperately for a patrol car. This was one time she would gladly face a policeman. Unfortunately none were around.

Desperation sank in. Maybe she should get out and walk. But hadn't her natural-childbirth instructor said that walking hurried labor along? What if she didn't make it far enough to find a ride to the hospital?

Through the light rain she spotted a pickup truck with a motorcycle covered in plastic in its bed. An insane idea struck her. Insane as it seemed, was it any crazier than delivering a baby in her car by herself?

Going with her instincts, Maddie awkwardly got out of her green convertible and waddled past two cars to the driver's window of the truck. She knocked on the foggy window.

The man inside turned his head to stare at her.

She smiled.

He didn't.

Maddie sighed and motioned for him to roll down his window.

"Yes?" he asked in a voice that sent a shiver down her spine. His radio played a heavy metal song, and it appeared there was someone in the passenger seat, but she couldn't be sure.

Maddie looked at the man and bit her lip. Though he was seated, he looked big and forbidding, and about as flexible as steel. His eyes were cool gray, his face angular and chiseled. Her longtime friend Jenna Jean was always telling Maddie that she jumped to conclusions about people, but this man didn't look friendly. He didn't look like he had much of a sense of humor. Under other circumstances she would turn around and go back to her car. The only thing she needed more than a sense of humor right now, though, was this man's motorcycle.

"I—uh—" Another contraction hit, and she held up her hand. "Just a minute, please," she whispered, and focused on the door handle. Inhale. Exhale. Inhale. Exhale.

Alarm cracked his features. "What in—"

With an effort she straightened after the peak.

"Does the motorcycle in the back of your truck work?"

"Yes, but—"

"I know this is unusual," she said in a rush, because she wanted to voice her request before another contraction hit. "But I'm in labor and I need to get to a hospital before—"

A gush of water spilled down her legs. Maddie stared at her drenched tennis shoes. "Oh, damn."

"Damn?"

"My water broke," she said, and met his wary gaze. Maybe he was human after all. When he wasn't glaring, he was almost attractive. She reassessed him. At second glance, he still looked a bit grim, but responsible, she thought hopefully. The strength stamped across his features appealed to her. And with those shoulders, she'd bet he had a killer body. In other circumstances she might have— Maddie looked at her watermelon stomach and dismissed the thought. "Can I borrow your motorcycle, please?"

The radio volume lowered. "Dad, who's standing outside—" The younger male voice abruptly stopped. "It's a pregnant lady," he said, his voice cracking in adolescent surprise.

Dad didn't answer his son's question. In one swift motion he was out of the car, staring down at Maddie. "Let me get this straight. You want me to take you to the hospital on a motorcycle?"

She nodded and covered her abdomen protectively. "I don't think I have much choice. I don't want to have this baby on Highway 81." When he didn't immediately respond, she felt a slice of panic.

What if he didn't help her? She clasped her fingers together. "Listen, I don't have a lot of money, but you can have it." He shook his head. "I'm a travel agent. Maybe I could arrange a free trip for you. Or I can cook," she said, feeling desperation thicken her throat. "I'll cook you a dinner a week for a year if you'll just—"

Another contraction hit, and the pain made her double over. In the middle of it she heard some tersely worded instructions. By the time the pain passed, the motorcycle was out of the truck, and the son had slid over to the driver's seat. Fighting tears of relief, Maddie gave the wide-eyed teenage boy a weak smile.

"Miss—" the man began awkwardly.

"Maddie, Maddie Palmer," she told him, extending her hand.

His large, warm hand swallowed hers. "Joshua Blackwell," he said, his face tight with concern. "Can you make it to the side of the road?"

She nodded. "Yes, thank you so much."

Joshua walked behind her. "Save your thank-yous for when you get to the hospital," he muttered, carefully placing a helmet on her head, then another on his, before he mounted the bike.

Maddie shot the motorcycle a doubtful look and gingerly straddled it. Motorcycles were not designed for pregnant women. Biting her lip, she stretched her arms around her bulk to his waist and held on tight.

"Are you on?"

"Yes," she whispered, wrestling with another contraction.

"How far apart are they?"

Maddie waited until the pain passed. "Under four minutes."

"Great," he muttered. "All I want you to do is hold on. I'm gonna move as quick and easy as I can. When you feel a contraction coming on, squeeze me, yell at me, kick me—just let me know."

Her opinion of Joshua rose ten feet. He was strong. He was practical. Most importantly, he was there. "Okay."

He nodded shortly and started the motor. "Let's go."

They made it to the hospital in seventeen minutes and thirty-two seconds. Joshua was counting. It must have been a helluva ride for Maddie. By the time they arrived, her face was pinched and drawn. She practically fell off the bike. The ER crew helped her into a wheelchair and took her up to delivery, shouting instructions at Joshua to follow.

He'd never been one to blindly follow instructions, but this time he did. Driving a red-haired pregnant lady to the hospital set his adrenaline humming. He washed up, dressed in a sterile paper coverall and was directed to the birthing room.

"Hi," she said, her voice laced with relief as he walked through the door. "They say my o.b. doctor won't get here in time."

He frowned. "What about your husband?"

"I don't have one," she said, and looked away.

Joshua took a long look at her. Her face pale against the drab hospital gown, she looked young and scared. Aside from the massive bulk at her midriff, her body was small-boned and delicate. He felt a strange wave of protectiveness, and despite the odd circumstances, assessed her again. Her breasts were full, her legs shapely. He couldn't venture a guess about her hips, since they weren't visible. But he would guess she was usually slim.

Freckles on her nose, wary curiosity in her brown eyes, she watched him watching her. The tilt of her chin told him she was a fighter. Something about her mouth told him she was a woman of passion, and Joshua felt a flicker of curiosity.

"You don't have to stay if you don't want to," she told him.

Struck by a rare moment of indecision, Joshua stifled a curse when Maddie closed her eyes and began to breathe deeply.

Her face crinkled in pain and she shook her head. "I need to push. Go get the nur— No!" she choked out and reached for him when he turned. "Stay."

He let her grab on to his hand. For a small woman, she squeezed him tighter than a vise grip. "Pant," he told her, dimly recalling his experience with the birth of his son sixteen years ago. "Pant."

Wonder of wonders, Maddie complied, panting until the urge to push passed. When Joshua tried to withdraw his hand, she shook her head, her eyes wide with fear.

His heart twisted, the sensation strange, nearly forgotten. "I'll be back in less than thirty seconds. I promise."

Her gaze meshed with his, and he saw the second

she trusted him. It gave him a rush, but he shook it off. He would have to think about that later. A baby was waiting to be born.

True to his word, Joshua returned swiftly, with a nurse in tow. Everything happened quickly after the nurse examined Maddie. "Don't push. You'll tear. I'll find the doctor."

"Where is he?" Maddie demanded. "Drinking coffee and eating donuts. I swear, men are never around when you need them."

Talking more to herself than anyone else, she grimaced as another contraction hit, cursing all of mankind. "You wouldn't think one little hole in—a— condom—" She broke off and sobbed. "Could-cause-this-much-pain," she finished in a rush.

"Maui," she murmured to herself. "S'posed to visualize something pleasant. Maui. If I were in Maui, I'd be snorkeling off of Molokini. I'd be—" She stopped and screamed. "Where is the doctor?"

Joshua took her hand and held it even when her nails bit into his skin. The doctor finally appeared, and Maddie pushed for twenty-three tense minutes before her squalling baby boy made his appearance. The nurse wrapped the baby and laid him on Maddie's chest.

"He's beautiful," she said, tears streaming down her cheeks. "He's just beautiful." She touched his pointy bald head and smoothed his crumpled ears. "You were in a hurry, weren't you?" she cooed.

The moment was so intimate it was hard for Joshua to watch. Suddenly feeling superfluous, he swiped the perspiration from his forehead and thought about making his exit.

The movement must have caught her attention. Maddie glanced up at him. Sniffing loudly, she smiled through her tears. "He's beautiful, isn't he?"

Joshua looked at the baby and twisted his mouth. "Yeah, he's something else."

"Want to hold him?"

Nonplussed, he hesitated.

"Go ahead," she urged, tilting the bundle toward him.

Joshua moved forward and gingerly took the baby in his arms. So small, so fragile, but so alive. He looked at the little human being staring back at him. The baby waved his fist in the air.

Joshua thought of Patrick. He'd always done his best for his son in his wife's absence, but during the long years of his struggle to do the right thing, something inside him had just died. Despite his best efforts, he knew Patrick had needed something from him that he just couldn't give. So it was with a great sense of shock, that after twelve years out in the cold, Joshua felt a rush of warmth. The sensation was so unfamiliar he didn't know what to do with it.

A nurse rushed into the room. "Ms. Palmer, the people you asked us to notify are in the waiting room and are quite insistent about seeing you. Mr. Benjamin Palmer—"

"My brother," Maddie said. "And I'll bet the other is Jenna Jean."

"Ms. Jenna Anderson," the nurse said.

"Tell them I'll see them in a few minutes and,"

she added, a trace of mischief mingling with the weary joy in her eyes. "Tell them I had quintuplets."

The nurse's jaw dropped, and she glanced at the baby in Joshua's arms. "Pardon me."

"It's just for fun," Maddie said. "They've agreed to be the godparents." She chuckled, then looked up at Joshua and the baby. Her eyes softened. "Bet when you woke up this morning you had no idea you'd be rescuing a pregnant lady from a sinkhole and helping deliver a baby."

"Can't say I did," he said, thinking she had more exuberance in her little finger than he had in his entire body. He felt the sting of envy and unwilling attraction. The double pop of unfamiliar emotion unsettled him. "Here he is," Joshua said, bending to return the baby to Maddie.

She held the baby against her chest in a natural maternal way. In a move just as natural, she extended one hand and urged Joshua closer. "Come here," she said, and surprised the hell out of him by kissing him right next to his mouth. "Thanks. You were a hero today."

He stared into her warm gaze and felt a weird shift inside him. Blinking, he backed away and cleared his throat. "No problem," he muttered. "I should go. You take care of the kid. And take care of you, too," he said, feeling a grudging acceptance that he was walking out of Maddie Palmer's life.

Joshua didn't remember the exact day he'd stopped dreaming. He just knew he hadn't dreamed during his sleep in years.

When Joshua slid between the covers of his big bed that night, he didn't expect any dreams. He listened to the silence in his house. It was a good silence, he told himself. Especially after the noise of the day.

He thought about the schedule he'd set for bringing in mares and getting them settled. He thought about his teenage son and how each day seemed to bring a little more distance between them. It disturbed him, but Joshua knew Patrick was growing up, and growing up meant pulling apart from his dad.

His mind eased back to the picture of Maddie with her newborn son, prompting a memory of the day Patrick was born. He and his wife had been far too young for the responsibility of raising a child, but they'd accepted that responsibility, anyway.

They'd both been full of hope and full of dreams.

That had been before Gail got sick. Before she faded away before his eyes and died. Patrick had only been four years old.

Sometime after that Joshua stopped dreaming. It was okay, he told himself. He had work to do, and he had to fumble his way through being a single parent. Life was serious business. For Joshua there was no time for dreams.

Two

Early evening at the Blackwell's ranch home, and it was quiet. Joshua thumbed through the newspaper. The only noises were restless noises, the rustling of his paper, his son's foot tapping against the kitchen chair as he did his homework, and his German shepherd, Major, prowling around the front door.

He was accustomed to the absence of noise. If he allowed himself to think about it, Joshua could nail the emotion the quiet provoked—emptiness. But Joshua was a busy man with the responsibilities of managing a successful horse farm and raising his teenage son by himself. There wasn't time to dwell on what was missing.

He glanced over his newspaper at Patrick. He suspected Patrick viewed him as a stern, humorless and cold man. A sliver of doubt cut through, and Joshua wondered if indeed he had become that kind of man.

Dismissing the unproductive thought, he glanced back at his paper and ignored the distance between his son and him. But the quiet, the endless, empty quiet, remained.

Major growled.

"Lay down," Joshua commanded.

Major obeyed for a quarter minute, then rose again and started barking. Patrick glanced up from his homework. "What's his problem?"

Joshua shrugged, getting up to let the dog out. As soon as he opened the door, he heard the distinctive sound of a muffler in need of repair. The muffler was attached to a car making its way down the dirt road to his house. Major was barking his fool head off as Joshua squinted his eyes against the evening darkness. He flicked on the outside lights. The car was vaguely familiar, but he couldn't quite remember...

The green convertible pulled to a jerky stop right in front of his house. A moment later the driver's car door opened, and the sound of a screaming baby joined Major's chorus.

Patrick joined Joshua. "What..."

The two Blackwell males watched in amazement as Maddie Palmer put her baby in a pouch she wore on the front of her, grabbed two large baskets and stomped past Major up the steps.

"Hi," she said cheerily, her brown eyes glinting with the same good humor as her uptilted mouth. "Remember me? You gave me a ride to the hospital six weeks ago and helped deliver my baby. I promised a meal a week for the next year, and I try to keep my promises. So, here's your first one.''

"Excuse me?" Joshua said, staring at her in disbelief. She didn't actually think he could have forgotten her. He sure as hell had never driven any other pregnant women to the hospital on the back of his motorcycle.

"Food," Patrick said, his voice nearly trembling with joy. "She brought food, Dad."

"This isn't nec—"

She lifted her shoulders in a half shrug. "Already done."

As the baby started to fuss, Joshua and Patrick took the baskets. "This really isn't—" Joshua began again.

"There's a pie!" Patrick shouted as if he hadn't seen one in years.

"Come in," Joshua said as the baby got louder.

"I underestimated how long it would take me to find you," she told him as she followed him toward the sofa. "Plus I got lost and had to ask one of your neighbors for directions. Mr. Crockett. He's a crabby one, isn't he?"

"You stopped at Otis Crockett's house?" Patrick asked, his attention veering momentarily from the food to Maddie. "Did he pull a gun on you?"

"He didn't exactly point it at me," Maddie said, freeing her fussing son from the pouch. "But he had it over his shoulder and he wasn't helpful. I told him he needed to work on his language. It could strip wallpaper."

"Oh, God," Joshua muttered under his breath,

feeling a thud of uneasiness in his gut. Maddie looked so helpless and Otis enjoyed firing guns. "Don't stop at Otis Crockett's house. He's been to court for his temper before."

"He needs a personality makeover," she said over the baby's wail.

"Don't stop at—" For emphasis, Joshua started to repeat himself, but broke off when he saw Maddie pull her shirt from her waistband.

His expression must have stopped her. She paused and lifted her shoulder. "Studmuffin, here, is way overdue for his feeding. I'm sure it's nothing you've never seen before, but—"

"In the kitchen, Patrick," Joshua said, immediately turning around and walking away. He rubbed the back of his neck and shook his head. Stifling an oath, he motioned for his son to sit facing away from Maddie as she nursed her baby.

"Dad, it's not that big of a deal. It's natural."

"Tell someone else, Patrick. I was sixteen once." He began to understand why most hurricanes were named after women. In less than two minutes, Maddie had walked into his quiet peaceful home and turned it upside down.

He pulled the dishes from the baskets and served the food, noting the baby's silence. That meant Studmuffin was being fed, and Maddie's breasts were bare. Nothing to get worked up about, Joshua told himself. As Patrick had said, it was natural. But it had been a long time since a woman had sat in his den, longer still since a woman with bare breasts had sat there.

Joshua deliberately cleared the image from his head and focused on the food. It was much better than the scrambled eggs he'd planned.

"This is great," Patrick said as he reached for another piece of fried chicken.

"Enjoy it," Joshua told him dryly. "It'll be your last great meal for a while."

"Not that long," Maddie said from behind him.

He jerked his head to look up at her, taking note of her rearranged clothing and then her smile. Her smile was slightly crooked, but generous and appealing enough to hold his attention. He lifted his eyebrows. "Not that long?"

"That's right," she said, as she gently patted the baby on the back. "I promised you one meal a week for a year."

He immediately rejected the idea. "That's not necessary. It was nice of you to bring this tonight, but let's call it even with this one," he said, ignoring Patrick's protest. "It's not practical or reasonable for you to bring a home-cooked meal all the way out here every week."

Maddie's smile grew wider. "It wasn't really practical or reasonable for you to drive a pregnant woman to the hospital on the back of your motorcycle, then stay with her during the delivery of her baby, either, was it?"

"I—"

"That's an excellent point," Patrick said.

Joshua clamped his mouth shut. Between his son, the bottomless teenage pit, and Hurricane Maddie, he could see he was going to have to be firm. "It's not—"

"I should leave," she said, gathering her basket and a few of the empty dishes. "Maui's a little temperamental, and since I don't know my way around your neighborhood in the daylight, let alone the dark, I'd hate to get stranded."

Thoroughly confused, Joshua stood. "Maui?"

"Oh, that's what I named my car. A couple of years ago I had to choose between taking a trip to Maui and buying a new car. I chose Maui and decided to call my car that as a reminder every time it broke down." Glancing down at her sleeping baby, she shook her head. "Didn't you hear what I told you last night?" she whispered. "You're supposed to wait for me before you go to sleep."

The baby didn't stir.

Maddie tossed Joshua and Patrick a wry glance. "Men."

Patrick laughed. "Did you, uh, really name him Studmuffin?"

Her eyes widened. "Oh, no. His name is David. A good solid name to make up for having an eccentric mother. Single mother," she added under her breath, and the light in her eyes dimmed just a little as if she knew the responsibility of raising a child would be a lonely venture at times.

She gave the appearance of being a damn-the-torpedoes kind of woman, carefree, full of husky laughter that made Joshua think of early mornings in bed. With her casually tossed red hair and mischievous brown eyes, a man might conclude she was a little wild. In his quiet, orderly world, she was noisy and disruptive. She was friendly, but she gave the impression she was at ease with her own sexuality. It was in the way she moved, the way she talked, the way she met his gaze. She made him uncomfortable.

"Like I said, I should go. Anything you don't like besides liver?" she asked as she headed for the door. "I aim to please."

Joshua felt a tug in his stomach and blinked. "Please," he echoed, his pulse kicking as his mind registered a swift, inappropriate, but scorching image.

She nodded. "Dinner next week. Thanks, Patrick," she said, walking onto the front porch.

"Thank you, Miss—"

"Maddie," she told him. "Just Maddie."

Joshua desperately needed to get control of the situation. "Let me take that," he said, and carried the basket to the car. A light drizzle fell. He opened the car door, and she fastened her baby in the car seat.

"Maddie," he began when she stood. "It was nice of you to bring the meal—"

"You're welcome."

Unaccustomed to being interrupted by a distractingly attractive woman, he paused a half beat before he got the conversation back on track. "It's not necessary for you to bring a meal every week. Not necessary, not practical, not reasonable."

She gave that husky chuckle again, and it shimmied down his nerve endings to flick across his masculinity. "Not practical, not reasonable. Thank goodness there are lots of things that aren't reasonable and practical. And I would argue about whether it's necessary or not."

She shook her head and leaned closer. She didn't intend it as an invitation. It was merely her natural body language, he knew, yet his fingers curled at the urge to just touch her. "I'm not used to being rescued by solid, dependable, conservative ranchers. I'm not used to being rescued at all. I need to say thank you. Do me a favor and just enjoy the meals. Okay?"

Speechless, he expelled a breath of frustration.

"I'll take that as a yes." She walked to the driver's side of the car and smiled just before she got in. "G'night, Joshua Blackwell."

"G'night," he muttered after she closed her door.

Her engine coughed to life, with the muffler buzzing loudly. He could barely hear himself think over the noise of her car, but he noticed Major started barking again, another animal howled in the distance, and the birds fussed at the interruption. Even the insects screamed as if they were on edge. Hell, the woman was an assault against nature.

In the evening mist, he watched her drive halfway down the lane. Her car rolled unevenly to a stop. It started to rain harder and Joshua sighed. The night wasn't over yet.

Maddie knew all too well why her car was listing to one side. She had a flat tire. "It's not all bad. This time I have a spare. And the baby is sleeping," she told herself, recalling that the last time she'd had a flat tire she'd held up a funeral procession and David had been fully, noisily, unhappily awake.

She pushed open her car door and stepped into a mud puddle. "This is just another one of life's adventures. It will make me a better person," she chanted under her breath. She'd been chanting the same verse the past ten years of her life and she was still looking forward to the day when she might actually believe it.

Rounding the corner of her car, she plowed into an immovable object. She blinked, then recognized Joshua. "Oh, bet you thought I was gone," she said with a sheepish smile. "You know what they say about bad pennies. Just can't get rid of them. You can go back to your house. I'm an old hand at changing tires."

She opened the trunk, and he grabbed the spare and jack before she did. Motherhood was making her slow, she thought irritably. "Listen, it's raining. I don't expect you to—"

"Why don't you sit in the car so you won't get wet? It won't take me but a minute," Joshua said, already kneeling beside the deflated tire.

Unaccustomed to having anyone do much of anything for her, Maddie felt uncomfortable. "This is really nice of you, but I can do it. You don't need to. You can—"

He looked up at her. "You sound like I did a few minutes ago."

Even in the dark the intensity of his gray eyes cut through her. Shutting her mouth, Maddie felt her discomfort grow. She'd never favored quiet men, especially those who refused to hold up their end of the conversation. She'd always preferred to spend her time with verbally expressive males, because she wasn't left wondering what they were thinking.

Joshua made her wonder. He was one of those salt-of-the-earth types who probably disapproved of her, but was either too reticent or polite to show it. And she would bet a year's supply of lottery tickets that he was a stick-in-the-mud.

A nice stick-in-the-mud, she amended because the man was changing her tire for her, but still a stick-in-the-mud. He looked like he needed somebody to loosen him up. She wondered if he had a sex life, if for that matter, he'd been kissed lately. The man looked like he needed a kiss.

Maddie felt a nudge of excitement at the same time she heard a warning bell. She was well familiar with the results of following that nudge of excitement. She'd gotten herself into trouble too many times to count, because she'd followed it. Well she wouldn't be fulfilling any kissing assignments for Joshua Blackwell, she told herself as she glanced in the car. She checked on David, who was still sleeping peacefully, then returned to Joshua's side.

She wished she had an umbrella handy to hold over him. Damp from the rain, his cotton shirt faithfully followed the contours of his broad shoulders, back and biceps. She would have to be blind not to appreciate the strength of his body. But the appeal was more than physical. For Maddie there was something insidiously seductive about a man who had clearly made it through some tough times.

Dependability. She swallowed her chuckle. Who would have ever thought Maddie Palmer would find dependability sexy? Her hormones must still be messed up from the pregnancy.

"Your son seems like a good kid. I bet you're proud of him," she said to break the quiet and interrupt her train of thought.

"Yeah," Joshua murmured as he continued working with the tire.

"Is he girl crazy yet?"

Joshua paused, glancing up at her. "If he is, he's keeping it a secret."

His voice was low and deep, wholly masculine, making her want to hear it more. How interesting, she thought, that a straight-and-narrow man could have such an appealing voice. "Academic type, huh?"

"Yeah."

She rolled her eyes. Stingy, stingy, stingy. "Plays his hand close to the vest?"

He nodded.

"Like his dad?"

He paused again and looked at her. "I guess so. I hadn't thought about it before."

That didn't surprise her. He didn't strike her as the kind to sit around and ruminate over his similarities with his son.

"You should have waited in the car," he told her as he lowered the jack. "You got wet."

Maddie glanced at her damp shirt. At the same time she knew her hair was probably sticking out in ten different directions from the moisture. She shrugged. "So did you."

He put the spare and jack in the trunk. "I thought women didn't like to get wet."

"Depends on the reason," she said. "Getting wet in the swimming pool or shower isn't bad. Getting wet because you're standing in line to get tickets for a concert isn't too bad."

He turned to her, and she could have sworn she saw his lips twitch. "What about getting wet because of a flat tire?"

His hair was damp, too, and for a fleeting second, Maddie couldn't help but imagine what Joshua would look like coming out of a morning shower. His body was clearly well-toned and muscular. The image dragged at her stomach, and she blinked to clear it from her mind. "Getting wet because of a flat tire? Depends on how much of an adventure it turns out to be."

His mouth tilted slightly, and he regarded her curiously. "Adventure in a dirt driveway?"

"Sometimes you have to make your own adventures," she told him, and sighed. "Now, how am I going to thank you for this? More meals?"

His eyes widened in dismay and she laughed. "Are you afraid of a bad penny? Do you want to put the flat tire back on?"

"No," he said immediately, without conviction.

"But you thought about it," she said, and laughed.

"How about a simple thank-you?" Joshua suggested.

The man looked like he needed to be kissed. The

impertinent thought nudged at her again, stronger this time. Well, darn, she thought, it wouldn't require anything monumental of her. But he'd said a simple thank-you would be fine. And some people actually preferred to lead calm, boring lives.

She nodded. "Thank you very much." The man looked like he needed to be shaken and stirred. Resigned to the inevitable, she stood up on tiptoe, touched his stubborn chin with her fingertips and kissed Joshua Blackwell on his hard mouth.

She heard his swift intake of breath and the surprise rippling through him. It reminded her of a kid taking cough medicine. Just a little longer for the medicine to work, she thought, and felt his lips test hers. His hand wrapped around the back of her waist. Maddie wasn't sure if he was urging her closer to him or holding her steady. Either way, she melted a little.

She was surprised at his response. Even more surprised at her own.

Her heart hammering against her rib cage, she pulled back and took a deep breath. Slowly, she backed into the open door of her car. "Adventure in a dirt driveway," she murmured. "I've never been good at doing anything the simple way, but thank you. G'night," she managed to say, then tumbled into her seat.

Three

Joshua stood in the rain staring after her long after the sound of her bad muffler disappeared. He stood there in the dark, in the mud, in the rain.

Like a fool.

He snorted and trudged toward the house. From the way he'd reacted, one would think he'd never touched a woman, let alone been kissed by one. Swearing under his breath, he rolled his shoulders. His damp shirt clung miserably to his skin.

Maddie Palmer was trouble.

Although Joshua didn't possess a great deal of experience with women, he'd always believed he had well-developed instincts.

Maddie defied those instincts.

She was a flake with a good heart. A flirt with good intentions.

Underneath it all, though, Joshua sensed a strong inner core of strength, and he felt a connection with her. In a way, she was like him. She would do what had to be done. But he wondered how she managed the easy smiles if she was half as scared as he'd been when he'd begun raising his child alone.

He thought back to how she'd nearly knocked the stuffing out of him when she'd kissed him. She looked good, smelled good, tasted good, but she wrecked the natural order of things.

The woman was trouble.

When Maddie pulled into her driveway, it was around ten o'clock. Her stomach was growling and David was waking up. Bone weary, she removed him from his seat and made her way into her town house apartment. "Okay, sweet Pete, I bet you're going to want to eat and play a little. Just let me get a ham sandwich," she whispered. "It won't take me but a minute."

Setting him down in the portable folding crib, she zipped into the kitchen. No sooner had she slapped mustard on two slices of bread, than the doorbell rang and David began to whimper. She poked her head around the corner and saw her brother walk through the door.

"Where've you been?" Ben asked and snitched the partially made sandwich from her hand. "I stopped by two times. I was starting to wonder if something had happened to you." He took a bite and made a face, looking at the bread. "What is this, anyway?"

Still unaccustomed to her younger brother checking on her every night, Maddie shook her head. "Right now it's a mustard sandwich. It had the potential to be a ham sandwich if you'd waited, but it was destined for my mouth," she said, plucking the bread from his hands. "Not yours. Do you mind holding Davey for just a minute while I finish fixing this?"

Ben glanced over his shoulder and gave a half smile. "Okay. But if he tries to nurse my arm like he did a couple of days ago, he's all yours."

Maddie touched Ben's arm and forced a mock-solemn expression. "Life is fragile. Since you're David's godfather, if something happened to me, you'd have to deal with him sucking on you, spitting on you, etcetera," she said. "All the time."

Ben got a slightly queasy look on his face. "I know. Why do you think I'm so concerned about your well-being?"

"Why? Because you love and adore me," she told him, and gave him a quick kiss on the cheek.

"Oh, give me the kid. He's easier to deal with than you are," he grumbled.

Maddie smiled to herself as she turned to finish fixing the sandwich and pouring some decaf soda. Ben sat on the couch, telling David about women in a soft, gentle voice. Her tough brother with the shoulder-length light brown hair, single earring, meticulously developed scowl and Harley in her driveway was a sucker for her baby.

She scooted into the den and situated herself on the end of the sofa so she could eat and feed at the same time. Taking a quick sip, she stretched out her arms. "I can take him now."

Ben shrugged. "Go ahead and eat. We're having a man-to-man, and he's fine."

"Okay. Thanks." Knowing she was on borrowed time, she stuffed the rest of the sandwich down and started on the soda.

"You didn't tell me why you were out so late tonight," he prompted, and stood when the baby began to fuss.

"Ten o'clock is so late?"

"For you, it is. You haven't been out much past eight since my bud here made his appearance." David began to root against Ben's arm again. "Oh, no. None of that. Here he is," he said, then quickly turned her son over to her.

Maddie laughed and discreetly adjusted her top to nurse her baby. "I took a meal to Joshua Blackwell and his son."

He looked at her incredulously. "You drove all the way past Catawba Mountain! In that disaster you call a car—"

"Maui," she said.

"And you didn't get lost?"

"I didn't say that. I got lost, but I eventually found his house. He and his son enjoyed the meal, and I left," she said. "After Joshua changed my flat tire." *And I kissed him.* Her brother didn't need to know that little fact, especially since it was an action she wasn't likely to repeat.

"You're not really gonna take a meal over there

every week for a year, are you? That's a little over the top even for you, Mad.''

"It is not. The man helped me when I needed it, and it meant a lot to me. I want to repay that in some way." Even if it drives poor Joshua crazy? She'd seen the expression on the man's face. She'd almost wondered when he was going to lift his fingers in a cross to ward her off.

"You get stubborn about the weirdest things," Ben told her.

Maddie glanced meaningfully at the python tattoo on her brother's forearm that had prevented him from getting several jobs. "I could say the same about you."

"That's different," he grumbled.

Maddie smiled. When Ben grew out of this rebel stage, he was going to be a great guy. She met his gaze affectionately. "Thanks for checking on me."

His brown eyes softened. "No problem. Call me if you need me."

"Have you talked to Mom lately?" she asked hopefully.

"The other day," he said. "Nothing new."

Maddie fought the stab of hurt. She knew what her brother was saying. Her mother still hadn't forgiven her for getting pregnant and having a baby when she was single. Maddie was beginning to wonder if her mother would ever accept David.

"Get some rest, Maddie," Ben told her.

She nodded. "G'night."

Within a moment the silence settled over her. Looking down at her son, she fought the sometimes

overwhelming fear that accompanied the silence. He
was so precious, she thought, marveling at him again.
So incredibly precious, and she was totally and completely responsible for his health, safety and well-
being. She caressed his fuzzy head and struggled
with tears. Many times she wondered if she was up
to the job. Not that she had any choice. She would
fight tooth and nail anyone who tried to take David
from her.

But still she wondered, and when she got tired of
wondering, she resolved that she would be up to the
task. She would learn to play baseball. Heaven help
David, she thought, because she couldn't hit the
broad side of a barn with a ball. She could in-line
skate, though, and she could teach him to dance.

More important than all that, she wanted to be able
to teach him to grow up happy and healthy. Believing in himself, able to give and receive, able to love
and dream. Loneliness was powerful, but love and
dreams were stronger.

Her mind switched to Joshua Blackwell and she
frowned. He made her wonder. She'd originally
thought he was a superstraight arrow. He either re-
pressed his needs or didn't have any, she'd con-
cluded. Maddie could hear her friend Jenna Jean
fussing at her for jumping to conclusions.

She grimaced. Jenna might have been right this
time. There was something unapologetically male,
unforgivingly driven about Joshua. It had taken a few
seconds, but he'd responded to her kiss. His mouth
had begun to move in sensual exploration over hers.
His chest had felt hard against her breasts. His thighs

had glanced hers, making her aware of his strength and masculinity.

His response bothered her, but what bothered her most was her response. She hadn't expected her pulse to race, or her breath to shorten. She would never have predicted her knees would dip.

Well, she'd learned her lesson. Underneath that calm, stick-in-the-mud surface, was a mystery man with the potential of a powder keg. She wouldn't underestimate him again.

Joshua took a hot shower to eliminate the damp chill that permeated his bones after changing Maddie's tire. After a minute or two spent mentally assessing the day, he usually drifted off to a dreamless sleep. Tonight, however, sleep eluded him. When he closed his eyes, he was more aware of his body than he had been in years. His skin, his heart pumping, his breath.

He got up and swallowed a rare, double shot of whiskey, then returned to his bed. After a little while the alcohol and quiet took the edge off his tension, and he closed his eyes. When he finally began to relax, a vision of Maddie teased his mind like a buttercup under his chin. Trouble—the woman was trouble.

But she was so warm, so alive.

Joshua sighed and gradually drifted off to sleep. And he dreamed.

Maddie smiled at Patrick when he answered the door. "Beef Stroganoff okay?"

His eyes lit up. "Yes. Come in, Maddie." He looked past her to the car. "Where's Dav—"

Sweeping past him to the kitchen, she set down her baskets, then pushed aside her slicker to reveal the top of her sleeping son's head in the front pouch she wore. "I didn't want him to get wet." She glanced around. "Where's your dad? Is this a bad time?"

"He'll be back in a minute. One of the mares is giving him a fit."

She should seize this opportunity, she told herself, and leave. She didn't really want to see Joshua again, anyway. Especially after that little overture she'd intended as a charity kiss had ended up doing crazy things to her hormones. "I don't need to stay. I can just trade dishes next week and—"

Patrick looked horrified. "You're not gonna leave, are you?"

Uncertain, she hesitated. "Well, I just wanted to bring the food. Between getting lost, having to feed the baby, and your dad changing my flat tire, I think I put a crimp in your regular schedule last week."

"I would catch he—" Patrick stopped abruptly as if some inner voice reminded him not to swear in front of a woman. "Dad'll want to thank you for bringing it."

"And try to talk me out of bringing any more meals," she muttered under her breath.

Patrick chuckled. "Yeah, but you don't have to do what he says."

Spoken like a teenager yearning for independence, she thought. She opened her mouth to respond, but the front door whooshed open and Joshua stomped in with a string of curses that would have peeled the paint off the walls.

Maddie blinked, looking at Patrick. She tentatively peeked around the corner. His head drenched, water droplets dripping from his nose, Joshua was tearing off a gray rain slicker. His expression darker than a storm cloud, he must have felt her looking at him, because he lifted his gaze to meet hers. Maddie's heart jolted. He didn't look happy.

What are you doing here?

He didn't ask it aloud, but he might as well have.

His intensity rolled through her, surprising her. The image of a powder keg poked at her again. "Hi." She gave a limp smile. "I just dropped off the meal. Hope you enjoy it. I was on my way out."

She moved toward the door, but he shifted slightly, blocking her way. "No need to rush," he murmured in his trust-me voice that reached under her skin. "There's a downpour right now."

"My windshield wipers work great," she said, and tried to edge past him. Unfortunately David took up a little more space than she estimated. She brushed against Joshua, then quickly stepped back.

"It'll be better if you wait. Have you eaten?"

Maddie hesitated, feeling trapped. "No, but I was going to—"

"Is there enough for three?"

"Not really," Maddie said.

"Plenty," Patrick called back.

Maddie frowned. No help from the son. She went

for the direct approach. "You're probably not in the mood for company right now."

He lifted an eyebrow, then gave a quick exhale of amusement mixed with exasperation. "Oh, you mean because I'm about ready to shoot a prize-winning mare because she's turning up her nose at my stud?"

"Still kicking?" Patrick asked. "Are you sure she's in season?"

Joshua shot his son a dark look. "She's in season. She's just a picky, ornery female. Hell, I'm beginning to wonder if she needs violins and scented candles."

Maddie shook her head in confusion. "Excuse me. I don't really know that much about horse farms. Don't you mainly just teach riding lessons and train horses?"

Patrick laughed.

Joshua almost smiled. He pulled off his boots. "This is a stud farm. We breed racehorses. I've got a triple-crown-winner stud. He's not young, but he can get the job done nicely. Owners bring the mares to me and I supervise the settling."

"Settling," Maddie repeated.

"Breeding. Impregnation," he added when she looked confused. "Consummation."

Maddie's eyes rounded. "Oh. So you're in the sex business."

Patrick made a strangled sound of amusement.

Joshua blinked. He tilted his head to one side consideringly. "I can't say I ever thought of it that way, but, yeah, I guess so." His gaze flicked over her from head to toe. His eyes held curiosity and something else that made her slightly uneasy. "Take your coat off and stay awhile. I'll wash up."

Maddie stared after him, then slanted a glance at Patrick. "Does he always give orders like that?"

Resignation warred with rebellion in gray eyes so like his father's. "Yep. And they usually get followed."

Maddie tucked that bit of information away. A strike against him, she told herself. Though she'd always been amused by arrogant men, she'd never been the least bit interested in getting involved with one.

Both Blackwell men encouraged her conversation during the meal. Maddie would almost swear Patrick was as hungry for feminine company as he was for food. He was an interesting kid, academically oriented, but he also enjoyed discussing music. Joshua didn't talk much, but she felt his gaze on her the entire time. It was just enough to keep her feeling disrupted.

They gave her privacy to feed David, then Joshua helped carry the dishes to her car. "The rain's almost stopped," he said. "Be careful. The lane might be slippery."

Maddie buckled Davey into his seat and slid his pacifier into his mouth. As she rose, Joshua stepped closer.

"I'm curious, Maddie," he said. "Do you kiss every man who changes a flat tire for you?"

Maddie tensed. "Well, to be perfectly honest, no man has ever changed a flat tire for me. I change them myself." She shrugged, wishing there was a teensy more space between them. "But it's true that I'm an affectionate person. I hug a lot, kiss on the cheek. I'm sure it makes some people uncomfortable. But you don't have to worry. I can tell you're not the touching type, so I won't be bothering you anymore by—" She took a quick breath, blew her bangs and looked away. Why did she feel embarrassed? "By kissing you."

Joshua was silent a long, uncomfortable moment. If he would just move, she thought, then she could duck into her car and—

"Bother." He rolled the word around in his mouth as if he was trying the taste of it.

Maddie looked up at him. His gray gaze studied her.

He nodded slightly. "Yeah, you bothered me when you kissed me. Did it bother you any?"

The hint of sexual challenge in his voice surprised her. She considered lying, but as in most things, Maddie always got caught when she lied. "A little," she conceded reluctantly. "But I didn't intend it that way. More as a thank-you and because I thought you hadn't been kissed in a while."

Joshua stared at her. The corners of his mouth slowly inched up. "That was a pity kiss?"

Maddie felt her face heat. Thankful for the cover of darkness, she silently swore. "A thank-you," she muttered.

"A pity kiss," he corrected.

Damn. She sighed. "It won't happen again."

"Why not?"

She ducked under his arm and quickly shut the car

door. "Because I don't think you need that kind of thank-you," she retorted, walking toward the other side.

"No more pity kisses for poor Joshua," he said, razzing her.

"No." Maddie pulled open the driver's side car door, but Joshua stopped it.

"That's a shame," he said. "Maddie," he prompted when she continued to stare at the car door and not look at him.

She reluctantly glanced up at him. "What?"

"Thanks for the meal." Then he closed the gap between them and pressed his mouth to hers.

There wasn't an ounce of pity in the gesture, Maddie thought, as her equilibrium went haywire. His mouth suggested and seduced, then he took her a step further when his tongue slid past the barrier of her lips and tasted her as if it was his right.

Her mind rebelled, but her body responded. She leaned into him, and her hands dropped to his arms, clinging to him. He wasn't rough. But she could taste his sensual curiosity and determination. His strength was tempered with gentleness. A potent combination, it got to her, slid past her defenses and took her breath. She could almost feel it knocking on her heart.

No.

That wouldn't do, Maddie thought. She couldn't open her heart to a man right now. She had to make a safe place inside and outside for her and her baby, and Maddie had learned that didn't include a man.

She pushed away from him and struggled for

breath. "I believe that's enough gratitude from either of us," she managed to say. "No more thank-you kisses. No more pity kisses. No more," she said, and swallowed hard. *Wow.* "I'll see you next week. G'night."

Not waiting for his response, she got into her car and drove down the lane, mentally chanting, *No more.*

Four

Joshua stood in the rain staring after her long after the sound of her noisy, nearly dead muffler disappeared. He stared after her. Again.

He felt like a fool.

Again.

Joshua cursed and vowed that he was not going to get all worked up over a flighty woman like Maddie Palmer. He refused to attribute the dream he'd had last week to her, the first dream in over ten years. It was probably the food, he reasoned, as he stood in the rain. His stomach was unaccustomed to decent food, so his digestive system had kicked his brain into overdrive, and that was why he'd dreamed that night last week.

Logical explanation, he told himself, since he hadn't dreamed since then, and the dream hadn't been about Maddie. For Pete's sake, it had been about buttercups, a field of buttercups. Joshua resolved to dismiss her from his mind, the sensation of her lips from his, her scent from his nostrils.

No more, and no more it would be.

Turning away, he glanced down at the ground, and a beam from the porch light caught an object near his feet. He narrowed his eyes and shook his head, swearing again. The night wasn't over yet.

Maddie retraced her steps from her car for the third time as she jiggled David in her arms. She'd fed him again after she'd arrived home, then planned to put him down. A vital part of his go-to-sleep routine was missing, however. Every time she thought she had him jiggled to sleep and began to lay him down, he whimpered. The whimper grew to a frustrated cry that progressed to sobbing that made her feel like someone had ripped out her heart and stomped on it. She was going to join him with the sobbing soon.

Returning to the house, she shook her head again. She knew she should have bought another one. Feeling the lateness of the hour pull at her, she sighed and paced across her den, humming as she tried to soothe him. "Sleep, sweetie," she whispered. "You'll feel so much better." She swallowed her laughter. "I'll feel so much—"

A knock at the door caught her by surprise. Ben, she predicted, and opened the door. She blinked at the sight of Joshua Blackwell on her front porch. Dressed in worn jeans and a leather bomber jacket, he stood with his hair slightly mussed, his eyes fixed on her. Her heart did a quick climb into her throat.

"Hello?"

"Thought you might need this before morning." He raised his hand and offered her the missing pacifier.

"Oh, my goodness!" Maddie felt as if she'd just been given the Holy Grail. "Thank you!" she said, scooping up the pacifier. Maddie was so relieved she didn't know what to say. Of course, that didn't keep her from talking. "He must have spit it out, and then it fell out of the car. I can't tell you how grateful I am. He wasn't going down, and I was beginning to wonder if either of us would get any sleep tonight."

When Joshua continued to look at her without saying anything, she fought the dipping sensation in her stomach. "Well come in and—"

He shook his head. "Not necessary."

"Yes, it is," she insisted. "You've driven far to deliver a pacifier. Let me fix you a cup of coffee or cocoa before you get back on the road."

He started to shake his head again, and Maddie's impatience zoomed. "Do we need to argue about a cup of coffee?"

Joshua paused and gave a dry chuckle. "Guess not."

Feeling Joshua behind her, Maddie walked to the kitchen and turned on the coffeemaker. She shifted David to her other arm so she could wash the pacifier.

"Want me to take him?" Joshua offered.

She swerved to look at him. "Are you sure?"

"Yeah." He cracked an almost smile. "He doesn't look too heavy."

Maddie slowly handed David to Joshua. As weary as she was tonight, she felt a mixture of relief and apprehension at giving David to Joshua. It was partly anticipation of going back to work in a couple of weeks, she thought, when she would be sharing David's care even more. "Thank you," she murmured, noticing that Joshua held David naturally. He didn't appear the least bit awkward. His large hands held him against his chest, securely, but not too tight.

Strong yet gentle again. Her body remembered being held by him, and Maddie felt that insidious melting sensation inside her, surprising her again. She hadn't known she was vulnerable to the combination. After all, her fiancé had been a here-today, gone-tomorrow musician. She'd been the grounded one.

It was a strange sensation having a man besides her brother in her home. Here in her little self-proclaimed no-man's land, his unapologetic masculinity reminded her she was more than a mom. She was a woman.

She blinked away that thought. "You look like you've done that a time or two."

"Yeah, it's been a while. He's almost asleep."

Maddie washed the pacifier and rolled her eyes. "It's a trick. As soon as I put him down, he wakes up."

"Does the pacifier help any?" he asked, keeping his voice low. The sound was oddly intimate, and it echoed inside her.

She shook off the odd sensation. "It's magic. I

wish everything about parenting were this easy. You have a problem? Go to the store and find something magic that costs under two dollars that will defuse any crisis."

"Scared?" he asked, surprise lacing the single word.

"Terrified," she said with a nod. "Does it show?"

He shook his head. "No. Not at all."

She took David from Joshua and her heart twisted as she looked at her sweet, trusting baby boy. "Well, I am," she whispered. "Scared spitless. Poor kid. He's got a mom who's hopeless in sports."

"Can you yell?"

She glanced at Joshua in confusion. "Yell? Yes, I can yell."

"Then you can cheer from the sidelines."

She smiled slowly, grateful this time. "Yes. I can do that." Coaxing the pacifier past his rosebud lips, she walked toward the upstairs nursery. "I have a few other—irregularities, though."

"Such as?" Joshua said from behind her.

Gently placing David in his crib, she lifted crossed fingers and counted to ten. "I think it worked," she whispered.

They walked down the steps together. "My long-time friend Jenna Jean who is an attorney puts it this way. I attract authority figures at unfortunate moments."

"Authority figures?"

"Traffic cops, meter maids and, just recently," Maddie added with a grimace, "the IRS."

Joshua winced too. "An audit."

Maddie nodded.

"Ouch."

"I've gone through different phases with this. I used to think it was bad luck. Then I decided it was timing that made the traffic cop give *me* a ticket instead of the guy who just passed me." She poured the coffee and gave him the mug. "I take responsibility for my little messes, but I do suspect there's some sort of karma at work here."

She thought about pouring herself a cup of coffee to do something with her hands, then remembered the caffeine and reconsidered. "I tend to bring disaster with me," she said.

"Uh-huh," he said, taking a sip and leaning his lean hip against her counter. "Bad luck. You're concerned you'll bring it on your kid, too."

Her heart tightened and she looked away. Maddie didn't want to think she'd bring bad luck to Davey, but sometimes when her defenses were down, she wondered.

"Or are you trying to warn me?"

She glanced up at him in surprise. "What?" Maddie wasn't sure she liked Joshua's knowing gray eyes. She supposed his being a stick-in-the-mud meant he wasn't easily fooled.

"Are you trying to warn me that you'll bring me bad luck?" he asked in a mild voice.

That hadn't been her intention. At least she thought it hadn't. "Why would I do that?" she asked, inhaling the combined scents of leather, coffee, and man.

"Because you got more than you bargained for with your pity kiss."

Maddie frowned. "Not that much more. It wasn't a big deal."

"Uh-huh," Joshua said, amusement mixing through his dry tone.

The sound was full of sensual challenge that she might have accepted another time. Maddie held his gaze, considering him. He didn't scare her, she told herself, though a shimmy ran down her nerve endings. As a rule, men didn't scare her. The exception being law enforcement officials. Men amused, irritated and charmed, but they didn't scare her.

It didn't matter, though, because now wasn't the time for a dalliance, even with a man like Joshua.

Now was the time for Maddie to get her act together for her baby and herself. She'd said *no more,* and perhaps subconsciously she was trying to reinforce it by talking about her bad luck.

"How has your luck been running since you met me?" she asked, winging it with his suggestion. "You were coerced into driving a pregnant woman on a motorcycle through the rain. You had to change a tire in the rain, and now you've delivered a pacifier, in the rain."

"Still trying to warn me off?" he asked with that sexy almost-smile on his face.

"You're a big boy," she told him with a little purr in her voice, unable to resist giving him back at least a little of his own. "I don't think I need to warn you about anything."

His gaze flicked over her, reminding her again,

with shocking clarity, that she was more than a mom. "Yep," he said, taking a final sip of coffee, "and I won't be warning you either."

He brushed against her as he set the mug on the counter behind her. Maddie held her breath. He backed away and she exhaled.

He nodded. "See ya next week. Thanks for the coffee."

She followed him to the door. "Thanks for bringing the pacifier," she managed to say, wondering how he'd switched gears so neatly. "I'll be able to sleep now."

"Grateful?" Joshua asked, cocking his head to one side. "How grateful?"

Her heart slammed into third, another gear change. She could keep up, she told herself. She was just a little rusty. "I'll bring dessert next week."

His gaze slipped over her again, a quick, hot and forbidden caress, before his expression became bland. "I'll look forward to it."

Assistant District Attorney Jenna Jean Anderson had an unflinching blue gaze that inspired fear, discomfort, sometimes hostility, but ultimately truth. It wasn't just something she pulled out for courtroom drama. It was part of her personality, and had been since her early childhood.

"You will tell the truth, the whole truth and nothing but the truth," she said, clearly softening her husky voice, a direct contrast with her forceful personality. "But if you don't like that nasty formula your mommy gives you, make sure you burp on her, not your godmother.''

She bent down and blew a raspberry on David's tummy. He smiled, and Jenna Jean grinned at Maddie. ''Better tell the neighbors to lock up their daughters. He's going to slay the ladies.''

''We're safe,'' Maddie replied. ''You're prejudiced. You won't be able to prosecute him.''

''He's adorable,'' Emily St. Clair Ramsey said as the three longtime friends shared lunch at her mother's well-appointed home. She squeezed closer to slide her finger under Davey's chubby chin. ''He's got your eyes and mouth and—''

''If you say he's got my body, I'm dumping this mimosa on your head,'' Maddie warned, lifting her goblet of champagne and orange juice in a mock toast.

Emily gave a surreptitious flick of her blond hair, but laughed. ''What a joke. You're slimmer than before the pregnancy.''

''Slimmer, not firmer,'' Maddie said glumly, then sighed. ''It doesn't really matter, though, because I'm not going to date until David turns eighteen.''

Jenna snorted. ''And I'm Tinkerbell.''

Maddie looked at her mimosa. ''No. I've thought about this. I don't want to be one of those mothers bringing uncles in and out of their children's lives.''

She sensed her friends' concerned gazes and looked up. ''With Clyde, I could accept the way he was here today and gone tomorrow because it was just me. It was okay, most of the time,'' she added with a sad smile, ''that he wasn't usually here when

I needed him. It was okay for him to pursue his dream in New York and California. If I was lonely, a phone call would help. If it didn't, I could call one of you. But I can't be that way anymore. I've got someone besides me to think about now." She bit her lip. "I really don't want to screw this up."

Emily's eyes softened. "Oh, Maddie, don't be so hard on yourself. You're going to be fine. I'm sure you'll find a man who falls for both you and Davey."

"Spoken like a recently married woman who has had her faith in the adult male gender fully restored," Maddie said, but couldn't contain a smile.

"I can't disagree with that," Jenna Jean said. "But I'm not sure a complete moratorium on dating is necessary."

Both Emily and Maddie looked at Jenna in disbelief.

"How many dates have you been on lately?" Emily asked mildly.

"I've been busy. Monster caseload—"

"You said that last year," Emily said.

"And the year before," Maddie added.

Jenna Jean quickly closed her mouth. "We weren't discussing me," she said in a semisnooty voice she used when she was trying to get past a sticky issue. "The point is, if a good man walks into your life right now, don't kick him out because of postpartum blues."

An image of Joshua Blackwell flashed through Maddie's mind.

Jenna's eyes narrowed. "Who have you met?"

Maddie blinked. Was her face that transparent? Or

was Jenna that intuitive? Perhaps a little of both. "Not really anyone."

"Oh." Emily smiled slowly. "Then tell us about this 'not really anyone.'"

Maddie thought of Joshua and her stomach turned a little flip. She took a sip of mimosa. "I haven't met that many new people lately except the man who helped deliver Davey."

Jenna perked up. "Oh, that's right. The rancher. What was his name? *J* something…"

"Joshua Blackwell. He runs a horse farm, a stud farm," she added, shaking her head.

Jenna snickered. "Stud farm? Bet there's a testosterone overload on that property."

Maddie couldn't disagree. "I take meals to his house once a week. I promised I would before he took me to the hospital on the back of his motorcycle."

Emily winced. "I still can't believe you did that."

"Better than having the baby on Highway 81," Maddie said.

"What's Joshua like?"

"He's the father of a teenage boy. Very responsible. Doesn't smile much. Very serious. Salt-of-the-earth type. Probably a stick-in-the-mud," she added, feeling as if she was stretching the truth.

"He doesn't sound like your type," Emily said, clearly disappointed.

"He's not," Maddie agreed, and squashed the little voice inside her that argued.

"Bet he's got a great body," Jenna said, looking

at Maddie as if she were going to poke the truth out of her.

"He does," Maddie conceded and paused. "He smells..." She hesitated, searching her mind for the proper description.

"Bad?" Emily wrinkled her nose.

Maddie shook her head. "No, not at all. He smells like leather and fresh hay and..."

"Horses," Jenna offered.

"Not really. I don't know what it is." She laughed. "It's a lot different than baby powder."

"Oh," Jenna said, the one word carrying a wealth of meaning. "Testosterone."

"It's all in the scent," Joshua told Maddie over dinner the following week. She'd brought spaghetti and meatballs, and he was enjoying her curiosity as much as the meal. Patrick had inhaled his meal and gone to his room to watch a show on MTV, and David was napping on a blanket, so Joshua had Maddie's undivided attention. He found he liked it.

He liked the way her brown eyes latched on to him and she cocked her head to the side while she listened. Her earrings dangled from her ears, and he flexed his fingers to restrain the urge to rub the shiny silver webs between his fingertips. He fought the same urge with her tousled auburn hair, glinting in the light. Maddie wasn't the only curious one. After the second dream he'd had last week, he was more curious about her than ever.

"The stud picks up the mare's scent and he's ready for action," he said, catching the faintest hint of a clean, spicy feminine fragrance that made him want to lean closer.

"You mean he just smells her and that's it?"

Joshua could tell that her nineties point of view was getting in the way of her understanding. "Not exactly all of it. Sometimes we have to let her get used to him, put him next to her for a day or so. We have to be careful, though, or he'll hurt himself trying to get to her."

Maddie shot him a doubtful look and sipped her tea. "Hurt himself? Isn't that a bit rash?"

Joshua wiped his hand over his mouth to hide a grin. "It's instinct. Pure, raw, animal instinct. When there's a mare around and she's in season, a stud's got one thing on his mind."

She seemed to consider that for a moment. "I guess I could say I've met some men like that."

He shook his head. The woman didn't have a clue, and for some reason he wasn't ready to admit he'd like to be the one to teach her. "Not like a stud. They paw the ground. They strut. I've seen one break through a fence, another kick through a barn wall. That's why we give them a long lead and watch them when they do the job."

Her eyes rounded. "You watch?"

"Sure. I'm getting paid to provide stud service, and it's my job to make sure no one gets hurt, including my stud. We tie the mare, but she can still do a lot of damage if she's skittish and kicks."

"You tie the mare," she echoed. "This is a lot different than I would have thought."

Voyeurism, bondage. He could practically see the

images roll through her mind. She didn't look appalled, more surprised, and intrigued. His gaze dipped to the swell of her breasts beneath the scoop neck of her burnt orange blouse. He was close enough to see a few freckles on her chest. He was close enough to touch.

He wondered if she was just as curious in bed, then immediately smashed that thought. "It's not S&M, Maddie," he assured her. "We're just breeding tomorrow's triple crown winners the safest way we can," he told her.

She nodded. "That makes sense. You strike me as a man who would choose the safe way. I wouldn't think you would get caught taking a lot of chances."

"I've taken a few wild chances," he said, remembering the three times he'd banked on odds instead of reality. "I prefer a calculated risk."

She looked at him skeptically. "Oh, really. Tell me."

Not totally comfortable discussing this subject, he worked his shoulders and leaned back in his chair. "I guess you could call Patrick a wild chance. He was conceived in my daddy's '73 Chevy."

She smiled. "And do you feel like you won with that chance?"

"Yeah," he said with a nod. "The bad part was what happened to Gail. She lost some blood and they gave her a bad transfusion with hepatitis. It made her sick and she died of it four years later."

"I'm sorry," Maddie said, reaching her hand toward his arm. "I bet it was difficult."

He looked away for a moment, thinking what a

sad time that had been in his life. "Yeah, it was."
He sighed, ready to move on to another thought.
"But there were a couple of other wild chances. I
won my stud in a poker game."

"You?"

Joshua didn't know what to think of her disbelief.
For some reason it chafed at him a little. "Yep. It
was late. We'd had a little too much to drink, and
this guy was determined to win. He didn't care about
the money or the stakes. He just wanted the win. He
liked high stakes, so he threw in his stud for the last
turn of the cards. Everyone said he was nuts."

He chuckled over the hand of fate. "The cards
were in my favor, and I've built my business on that
win. The only other wild chance was buying this
place. It was a mess, but that was more of a calculated risk. It had more to do with working long hours
after the sun went down."

She shook her head, still smiling. "I don't know
what to say. You just seem so solid, so dependable."

He nodded and turned his hand over. "Yep. You
wanna finish reading my palm, Gypsy? You remind
me of a gypsy."

"Me?" Maddie laughed. "Okay. I'll do it no
charge this time, but don't expect it again." Skimming her fingertips over his palm, she told him,
"You're careful."

His gaze was caught by the gentle, rhythmic motion of her hand. It didn't make a damn bit of sense,
but her fingers soothed something inside him at the
same time they excited him.

How long had it been, he wondered, since a

woman had touched him this way? He wondered how her fingers would feel on the rest of him, seeking and pleasuring. He wondered how her naked skin would feel beneath his hands. He wondered what kind of sounds she would make. He wondered...

"Determined. You're one to make things happen," she said. "And you're not the kind of man to spend a lot of time dreaming."

Joshua felt the punch of her assessment in his gut. Not the kind of man to spend a lot of time dreaming. He hadn't missed dreaming, he reminded himself. It had suited him just fine. He pulled his hand back and rubbed it against his thigh. "Right again. I'm not a dreamer."

Five

Maddie wondered why he'd pulled back so quickly. "I didn't mean no dreams at all," she told him. "That would be a little extreme."

"Not really," he said in a mild voice, but he seemed remote.

Puzzled, she frowned for a moment, then gave a half laugh to herself. "Maybe I should leave you one of my earrings tonight."

Joshua looked at her as if she had a screw loose. "Your earring?"

"Yeah, it's a miniature dream catcher. Good dreams pass through the center, and bad dreams are trapped in the web until they disappear."

"All that in an earring," he said wryly.

Maddie pulled her earring loose and dangled it toward him. "Need a little help with your dreams?"

"No."

His response was a shade too fast, she thought. Was it possible that Joshua had a weak spot? She studied him again. Not a pretty face, he had a tough jawline and mouth, and eyes that narrowed in doubt. The tough-looking mouth was deceptive, she remembered with a trace of discomfort. Nothing fanciful about this guy. On the outside he was all strength and hard angles. She'd thought he would be the same on the inside, but she was learning Joshua was far more complex.

"What were you like when you were a kid?"

He shrugged. "Like most kids."

She rolled her eyes. "Stingy answer," she muttered, and sighed. "I'll be more specific. What did you want to be when you grew up? What was your favorite penny candy? What was your favorite toy?"

He hesitated. "I wanted to be a professional baseball player. A pitcher. I played through high school and would have played in college, but Patrick came along and I took a different road. My favorite penny candy was fireballs, and," he said, nostalgic amusement gentling his rough features for just a second, "I had this plastic Godzilla monster that roared."

Ah, she thought, so he *had* dreamed. Maddie smiled. "We would have never gotten along as kids," she told him and decided to "forget" her earring on the table. "I hated baseball. I wanted to be a rock star. I hid in my closet after I watched horror movies, and I would have fought you for the fireballs."

He cracked a grin. "So you were a troublemaker even as a child?"

Maddie shook her head and looked down her nose at him in a mock serious glance. "No. I've just always had unfortunate timing with authority figures."

"Uh-huh."

The sound of disbelief was sexy in an uncalculated way, and the thought of Joshua with dreams tugged hard at her heart. She understood about dreams that didn't come true.

Feeling a soft spot inside her form, she abruptly cut off her thoughts.

"I get caught," she told him and stood, flexing her resolve, and adding her next statement as much for herself as for him. "But not all the time." She was not going to get caught by any silly feelings for Joshua Blackwell.

That night Joshua avoided getting stuck in the rain staring after Maddie as she left. If he were a superstitious man, he'd think she brought the rain with her, because every time the woman came around it rained. Tonight, though, he didn't get wet, didn't change any tires, or find any pacifiers.

He didn't get kissed, either. That was okay, he told himself. He'd lived without Maddie's kisses for thirty-three years and he'd managed just fine.

He was pretty pleased with himself until he saw her earring on the kitchen table. Staring at it a moment, he picked it up and rubbed it between his fingers. The light reflected off the shiny silver, and he remembered the way the earring had bounced with each movement of her head.

She wanted to think of him as a dried-up old codger with no interest in the opposite sex. No interest in sex. That didn't sit well with Joshua. He shouldn't care, but he did. He was having a tough time resisting the urge to show her just how interested he could be.

He was having a tough time not putting his hands and mouth on her and learning what it took to change her perspective. She was a sensual woman, a feminine feast after a long fast. It was as if he'd forgotten to eat lunch, and it hadn't bothered him until Maddie called it to his attention.

She made him feel dissatisfied.

He pushed the sensation away, but the next morning when Joshua awoke, he immediately knew he hadn't dreamed. He felt oddly cheated.

"You did what?" Joshua demanded. The woman had gone way too far this time.

Maddie's eyes widened, and she held out her hands to Patrick for David. "I volunteered you to chaperon a dance at the community center."

"Why in hell did you—"

Maddie covered the baby's ears and frowned at Joshua. "Could you help me with something in the kitchen please?"

In a rotten mood, he tore off his raincoat. "I don't see why—"

"Ple-e-ease."

He inhaled deeply, his patience stretched. "Okay,

but if you're concerned about me singeing your baby's ears, you might want to leave him with Patrick.''

Maddie glanced at Patrick. "Do you mind?"

"Nuh-uh," he said, his expression one of relief that he didn't have to face his father.

"Thanks," she murmured, giving him a reassuring smile.

A premature reassuring smile, Joshua thought darkly, and led the way into the kitchen. He ignored the inviting aroma of beef stew and leaned against the counter. "Well?"

"While you were outside, Mrs. Quackenbush came to the door with her daughter and was selling tickets for the dance at the community center." She lowered her voice. "Have you seen Mrs. Quackenbush's daughter, Amy? She's very cute. She was looking at Patrick, and he was gawking at her, but was too shy to say anything, so..."

"So?" he said in a voice that sounded belligerent to his own ears.

Unfazed, she continued. "So, when Mrs. Quackenbush said they still needed some chaperons, I thought if you went it would give Patrick an opportunity to talk with Amy."

"It's a lousy idea."

She looked affronted. "It is not. It will only require a few hours of your time."

"How do you know I'm not busy that night?"

"I asked Patrick."

"I'm sure I've got something I need to do." If he didn't, he'd sure as hell find something.

"Oh, right," she said sarcastically. "You could always stay home, read the paper and watch the grass grow. This won't kill you."

"That's debatable," he muttered, his stomach growling along with his disposition.

Her eyes darkened with temper. "You know," she said, "the way you're acting, I'd almost think you're scared."

She was all dare, and he felt the kick of her challenge all the way down to his stomach. He resisted, barely, the urge to shut her tempting, impertinent mouth with a kiss. "I don't like other people making decisions about my schedule."

That took a little of the huff and puff out of her, he noted. She hesitated, then moved to the pot of stew and poured a bowl for him. "Well, you don't exactly have to go alone."

"Is that so?"

She was nervous for approximately thirty seconds before she grew impatient with herself.

Watching her toss the ladle into the pot, Joshua smothered a grin.

"Yes, it is," she said, and met his gaze with brown eyes that said "Don't mess with me." "I told Mrs. Quackenbush I would come with you."

Maddie considered herself a fairly tolerant individual. She knew she had a temper, but she tried to live by the philosophy that there was room for everyone and most everything if everyone made a little room.

Room for everything...except country music when

it was performed by a group of musicians who hadn't quite mastered the concept of "picking up the rhythm."

She could accept its current broad-based appeal, but Maddie was a rock 'n' roll baby from way back. When she'd volunteered to help chaperon with Joshua, she'd had no idea she would be trapped listening to hours of country music and watching line dancing. It was cute and fun for the first thirty minutes. After that it began to wear.

The band started another twangy song with a tempo appropriate for the dead, and she longed for Bruce Springsteen as she and Joshua held up the back wall of the community center.

"You're twitching again," he said, next to her ear.

"I'm not twitching," she retorted, rolling her shoulder at the rush down her nerve endings. "It's my body's natural response to a too-slow rhythm.

"Told you this was a lousy idea."

"We're almost halfway through."

"One-third of the way," he corrected. "These things last at least three hours."

Maddie did twitch then. "Does the band ever take a break?"

"Maybe somebody will break some strings or something."

She glanced at him and chuckled. "It's like pulling teeth to get you to have a little fun, isn't it?"

He looked at her in mild disbelief. "Is that what we're supposed to be doing?"

"You know, Joshua, you look pretty good tonight, but you have a terrible attitude."

"I told you I don't like my schedule being decided for me."

"It wasn't decided. It just got a little assistance."

He paused a half beat, then glanced at the dance floor. "How good?"

Maddie blinked. When realization dawned, she couldn't keep from smiling. "You look very good," she told him. His Western-style white shirt showed the contrast of his dark complexion and drew the eye, particularly the female eye, to his broad shoulders. Add that to the way his black jeans emphasized his height and very nice backside, and Maddie suspected half the women in the room were secretly drooling.

"In fact, there are a couple of women on the other side of the room who haven't been able to take their eyes off you. Have you thought about asking someone to dance?"

"I don't think I need to up my torture quotient tonight."

Maddie sighed. "I'm curious. How long have you been so..." She searched for a nice term and couldn't find one. "Crabby?"

He looked momentarily disconcerted, then his face cleared and he glanced his watch. "About an hour and fifteen minutes."

"No, no, no," she said, shaking her head. "I was thinking more in terms of years. And I wondered," she continued, "if it's related to a physical problem. You know like women have PMS?"

He wore that you-must-have-a-screw-loose expression on his face again and said, "PMS?"

"I've heard men experience something similar,

but it doesn't necessarily have to be a monthly thing." She lowered her voice. "Prostate problems. I understand a backup can cause irritability."

He looked stunned. "And you think I have a back-up?"

"Well, Joshua," she said, and she truly wasn't trying to insult him. "You probably don't realize this, but you're cranky. When Mrs. Quackenbush brought the tickets, I thought it might be good for both you and Patrick. You, to get out among people instead of horses, and Patrick needs to get some exposure to girls in a social setting."

With a sinking sensation, she realized by his dark expression, he wasn't receiving her suggestion with an open mind. Oops. In over her head again. "But this backup thing is just a theory, and you might not—"

"Excuse me," a man said, interrupting her massive backpedaling effort. "Would you like to dance?"

Maddie smiled with relief. Saved by the bell, or in this case, a slightly older man who wanted to two-step. "Thank you. That sounds very nice. I'll be back in a few," she told Joshua, feeling his gaze on her as she accepted the other man's arm and moved to the dance floor.

Joshua stared at the red-haired madwoman as she chatted up Henry Krause and danced to the dragging tune played by the band.

Backup.

In his prostate, for God's sake.

He swore under his breath. If there wasn't a grain

of truth to it, he'd be laughing himself silly right now. But he'd been thinking about Maddie a lot lately. In the barn, at the dinner table, in his bed. He still hadn't dreamed again, but he'd envisioned her in his bed, her arms wrapped around him, her body bare and susceptible, her mouth responsive. His thoughts had left him hot and hard, restless and wanting.

Joshua felt his crotch swell and swore again.

She wasn't beautiful, he tried to tell himself. She wasn't the most seductive woman on the face of the earth. She wasn't— Something inside him protested. She might not be the most beautiful or seductive woman, but she was the most interesting, vibrant, sexy-without-trying woman he'd met in his life. He wanted her. He knew he shouldn't do a damn thing about it.

He shouldn't, he reminded himself as the band finally took a break. Somebody didn't waste any time changing the tempo. John Cougar Mellencamp burst out loud and strong, singing "Hurts So Good." Joshua was still telling himself he shouldn't, when he watched in shock as his son asked Maddie to dance.

She nodded and laughed, swirling, twirling and singing along. The little skirt of her dress fluttered and flirted above her knees, grabbing his gaze, making him wish it would fly a little higher so he could see her thighs. Her hair bounced, swooping over her cheek, hiding one eye. Her shoulders shimmied making her breasts sway. She was just having fun, he told himself, but her abandon made him burn.

The song ended, and Joshua took a breath, expecting Maddie to return. But someone cranked up another rock 'n' roll number, and he watched a high school stud convince her to dance with him. Three songs later he was starting to feel impatient, restless...possessive. He snorted at the thought.

When a Tracy Chapman song oozed through the speakers, though, Joshua pushed away from the wall. It wasn't rational but he had given up on being rational at least for the moment. Making a path through the crowd, he caught her gaze, and she stared back at him.

"My turn," he told the hopeful high school kid, then turned to Maddie. "Dance with me." He took her hand in his, then put his other hand at her back and drew her closer.

"I didn't know you could," she said in a husky voice. "I thought it was against your policy to have fun."

He inhaled and drew in her spicy sweet scent. Her hair was soft under his chin. Her body was warm, and she moved in rhythm with him. "Maybe I need a little help."

"Having fun?"

Joshua kept his laughter to himself. His arousal, however, was another matter. "That'll do for a start."

Maddie shot him a questioning glance. "It'll do for a start?" Someone bumped against her, rubbing her body closer to his.

Joshua groaned.

Maddie was suddenly, completely aware of what

kind of fun Joshua was referring to. After dancing with high school kids, it felt unbelievably good to be held by Joshua. His thighs brushed against hers, and with each movement she was conscious of his masculinity.

He was focused intently on her. She could see it in his eyes, feel it in the way he held her. His fingers laced through hers, while his other hand at her back kept her just close enough to mess up her breathing. A seductive trap. She deliberately took a deep breath. "So what tripped your trigger? Mellencamp or Prince?"

"Neither," he said, and rubbed his fingertips over her spine.

Maddie felt her breasts swell. She fought her response. "Joshua," she managed to say, "did you know you're looking at me like Sylvester looks at Tweety?"

A slow, predatory smile tilted his lips. "You make me hungry, Maddie."

His lower body slid against hers again, and she felt herself go warm and liquid inside. The man pulled her to both ends of the spectrum. He was so solid and dependable that she was lulled into believing she could relax with him, but at the same time he played havoc with her respiratory system.

She swallowed. "Hungry," she repeated. "That's why I bring you meals once a week." Lame, she heard in the back of her mind. Lame, lame, lame.

"Oh, lady." He rubbed his mouth over her bangs in a sweet, hot caress. "I'm not talking about food."

Six

"It's not me," Maddie whispered desperately, her heart pounding double time. "You've just been cut off from normal society so long that exposure to any woman would—" She swallowed. "Affect you."

He dipped his head. "Do you really think I'd react this way to Mrs. Quackenbush?" He asked the impertinent question in the same intimate voice that made her knees lose their stiffness.

Maddie paused. Mrs. Quackenbush appeared nearly twice Joshua's age and probably weighed the same as he did. "Okay, maybe not any woman, but—"

"You're right," he said, his gaze wrapping around her. "Not any woman. You."

Her heart stopped. She missed a step, and for once in her life, Maddie was speechless. She half wondered if he was going to kiss her right there on the dance floor, but he didn't. He just held her and looked at her and let his words sink in.

The song ended, and another teenager strutted up for a dance. Maddie clung to Joshua a few seconds longer before she realized what she was doing. She blinked, releasing him. "Thank you," she murmured to Joshua, and watched him walk to the back of the room. Still staring after him, she automatically began to move when the music started again.

She wasn't used to this kind of attention from a man. Her longtime pseudo fiancé had been fairly casual about his desire for Maddie. She had been more of a stabilizing force in his life than his great passion. His great passion had been his music, and though his absences had left her feeling lonely at times, she had adjusted.

Maddie had told herself she didn't need to be anyone's great passion. Enduring friendship, companionship and respect were more important. She felt a pang at the memory of Clyde. The last time he'd gone back to Los Angeles, he'd promised to bring back a ring next time. It had always been "next time." She missed him, but for some reason he'd never been around when she'd truly needed him, so she'd learned to get along without him.

Joshua didn't strike her as the kind of man to cut out when the going got tough. The notion that he wanted her, not just any woman, rocked her little no-man's land. She couldn't remember being wanted with that kind of intensity. It stole into her heart and roused all kinds of secret, foolish wishes.

Two hours later Maddie and Joshua left the dance.

"Where's Patrick?" she asked as they approached Joshua's truck.

"He's coming home late tonight. Going to a fast-food place with some friends." He opened the passenger door. "So it's just you and me since your brother is watching David."

Maddie climbed into the seat. "So it is," she murmured.

He entered from his side and headed for his house where Maddie had left her car. Acutely conscious of his closeness, she rolled down the window to create the illusion of space, even though it was early spring, and the temperature was a little cool.

"Too warm?" he asked.

"Not really. I like the breeze."

Silence. It seemed to wrap around them and bind them closer together. Maddie couldn't stand it. "On a scale of one to ten, what would you say was the torture quotient for this evening?"

He glanced at her, then back at the road. "The evening's not over yet."

Her stomach dipped. "Then for the dance?"

He shrugged. "I give it a four with ten as the worst. I didn't have to dance with Mrs. Quackenbush, and Patrick finally got around to dancing with Amy."

Maddie nodded. "It took him a while, but when he finally got around to it, he didn't have any trouble."

"Bet you thought that since his father is a recluse—"

"I didn't call you a recluse," she protested.

"A social outcast," Joshua continued. "A modern-day monk—"

"I didn't say any of those."

"Nope," he said agreeably. "But you thought them."

She opened her mouth to protest, then hesitated and snapped it shut.

"I may be a recluse and a social outcast, but I'm no modern-day monk."

"I never said that," she repeated. "To be perfectly honest, I never even thought that one."

"Okay. What words did you choose?"

Maddie looked out the window and grimaced. How did she get herself in these predicaments? She went with his positive attributes and hoped that would be enough. "Solid, dependable, serious."

"And?"

She grimaced again. "Cranky and a stick-in-the-mud," she muttered in a low voice.

He gave a rough chuckle as he pulled into his drive. "Can't be all bad. It made you give me a pity kiss."

She felt her cheeks heat. "I thought we'd already discussed this." She frowned when she noticed he drove past the house. "Where are you going?"

"To the top of a hill. You'll like it. It's a clear night, and you can see the stars."

He wound around on a curvy dirt road, then pulled to a stop at the top of a hill. "C'mon out," he urged, and was at her door within seconds.

"Nice manners," she said as he helped her. "How did that happen?"

"Automatic response. My father isn't the most educated man, but he demanded respect and politeness from his kids."

"You see him much now?"

"Nope. I was the oldest and was offered a baseball scholarship to college, but since Patrick came I couldn't go. They were disappointed and then disappointed again when I moved here from Kentucky."

Maddie sighed, feeling a connection with him. "Disappointment's hard to live with sometimes."

"Yeah. I guess I was always too busy to worry about it much. It bothered me until I realized that maybe we both let each other down. I didn't do what they wanted. They weren't there for me when I needed them."

She looked at him in surprise. "That's pretty impressive."

He gave a half smile. "For a stick-in-the-mud social outcast?"

"Yes. My mother's not speaking to me right now. She thinks I should have given David up for adoption." She breathed in the cool air and looked at the stars. They looked like a million diamonds on a blue-black blanket.

"Has she seen him?"

"Pictures. My brother showed her some pictures."

"Her loss."

Maddie shook her head. "Everyone loses in this situation."

"Yeah, but she loses more. She doesn't get to hold her grandson, and," he said, moving closer to her, "she's missing out on you."

"I hadn't thought of it that way."

"Nope. You're too busy feeling ashamed."

She shook her head in surprise again. "For a humorless social outcast, you sure know a lot."

"Oh. We've added humorless."

She covered her mouth. "Oops. Who said that?"

"You're cold," he said, noticing her slight shudder. "Time to get back in the car."

Reluctant to leave, but growing cooler, she returned to her seat. "If I lived someplace like this, I'd probably climb this hill every night to look at the stars."

"Not when it rains."

"But I bet it's pretty when it snows," she told him, and craned her neck to look out the front window. "It's so quiet, peaceful."

"It is."

The deep tone of his voice got under her skin. Looking at Joshua, Maddie sighed and leaned back in her seat. "Thank you for bringing me here."

He cocked his head to one side, studying her, and his mouth tilted with a hint of a grin. "No thank-you gestures?"

Maddie's heart tightened at the dangerous expression on his face. "You mean kisses?"

"Uh-huh." He leaned closer.

It was amazing how sexy he could make uh-huh sound. She smiled because nothing was going to happen. She was certain. "Joshua, you're not the kind to be kissing women in your car."

"Is that so?" He lifted his hand to her hair.

Her confidence dipped a little. "Yes, it's so. You're practical and dependable and—"

"And I want you."

Maddie's breath stopped. "Somebody must have spiked the punch," she said breathlessly. "How much did you drink, anyway?"

Joshua shook his head and leaned still closer. "This isn't whiskey talk, Maddie. It's me, and you're wrong. I am the kind to be kissing you in my car."

She was all set to point out that she'd said *women* in a general sense, not specific, but his mouth covered hers. She felt his fingers slide beneath her hair to the nape of her neck.

Warm and inviting, he swept the tip of his tongue over the seam of her lips. Her stomach fluttered at the gentle pressure. She inhaled his scent and felt dizzy. It was so easy to respond, to rub her lips against his and learn the taste and texture of his mouth. When he gave a nearly inaudible groan, it was so easy to open her lips and test his tongue with hers.

He continued his gentle, sensual massage on her neck, but his mouth grew more avid, and suddenly the temperature in the truck jumped several degrees. Leaning into him, Maddie opened her mouth wider to accommodate his probing tongue.

Reeling from the sensation of falling, Maddie braced her hand on his chest. The kiss went on and on until Joshua pulled back, slightly, to take a breath.

His eyes burned with desire, and he shook his head. "Lady, you are something else."

He lifted his fingers to her lips, and she closed her lips around one. He closed his eyes briefly as if in pain, then opened them and watched as she took his index finger inside her mouth.

It wouldn't go too far in a car, she told herself. Maddie suckled his finger, not wanting to stop.

He swore. His gaze fell over her, lingering on her lips and throat, then her breasts.

He hadn't touched them, but Maddie felt her nipples tighten. She would almost swear there was an electric current humming in the air. A bare electrical wire too close for safety.

It sent off a warning bell in her system, but Joshua leaned close again, and all she could hear was the thumping of her heart. He pressed his open mouth against hers, rolling it from side to side, more sensual tease than kiss.

He made her want more.

He slid his finger down her throat to the top of her breasts, skimming his finger back and forth. "Every man at that dance," he said against her mouth, "was wondering what was under this little dress."

Feeling as if she were turning to liquid, Maddie swallowed. "Just the regular things. Bra and under—"

He gently bit her lip, and she sucked in a quick breath. He kept up the maddening skimming of his finger across the tops of her breasts. A restless sensation flicked at her nerve endings. She wanted him to touch her.

Closer, he moved his finger and lured her tongue into his mouth. Closer again, and she arched toward him. *Touch me. Touch me.*

His finger dipped beneath the satin cup of her bra and glanced her swollen nipple. A little moan bubbled up from her throat. The sound must have shredded another layer of his control. He stopped playing with her tongue and took her mouth in earnest. Within seconds her back zipper was released and the bodice of her dress was pushed down.

He rubbed the tight, sensitive tip of her breast between his thumb and forefinger, and she felt a corresponding thrumming in her womb. She moaned again, clutching at his shoulders and kissing him back with equal intensity. She felt his heat beneath her fingers, sensed the deep, needy thud of arousal pounding through him.

Everything he was doing, every move he made, tightened the tension inside her, and Maddie was so aroused she was spinning from it.

Pulling his mouth from hers, he took another breath. His eyes reminded her of the sky during an electrical storm. "I want to touch you," he told her. "Everywhere." He pushed the cups of her bra down and looked at her bare breasts. "You're so beautiful."

He cupped her, still taunting the tips with his thumbs.

Maddie pushed against him, needing to quell the ache. He gently squeezed, then lowered his head and took her into his mouth.

The sensation was so erotic she closed her eyes.

For the last year her body had been devoted to growing and nurturing a baby. Joshua reminded her she was a woman, with needs, the need to touch and be touched, the need to want and be wanted.

His features softened by moonlight, he suckled her nipple, and the ache inside her grew worse instead of better. "Ohhhh," she moaned.

Tugging at his shirt, she fumbled but managed to loosen his buttons. She ran her hands over his chest, her fingers luxuriating in his defined muscles and silky hair.

He made a rough sound of pleasure, then lifted his head. "This isn't enough." He pushed the seat back and pulled her onto his lap, then slid his hands up her thighs to where she was damp and needy. Through the panty hose, he rubbed her, making her wetter, making her ache more.

Restless, Maddie shifted in his lap, feeling his hardness against her hip. She wanted to touch him there where he was swollen with wanting her. She wanted to bring him the pleasure of her hand. She wanted…him.

She made a sound of frustration, and he squeezed her thigh.

"What is it?"

"I want— I need—" She closed her eyes. "Ohhhh!"

"I hate panty hose," he told her. "You've got too many clothes on."

Maddie tried to sit still, to make the havoc in her mind quiet. She tried to make the car stop spinning. "I'm wearing less than you at the moment."

He was all concern, closing his arms around her.
"Are you cold?"

"Not exactly," she managed to say, feeling as if
her skin was on fire. "Joshua, we are in a truck."
She couldn't believe it.

"Yep. It's a little restricted for what I want to do
with you."

He pulled her against his chest and nuzzled her
hair. The gesture should have helped to calm her, but
Maddie felt like a whirling dervish on the inside.
Edgy, rattled, needy. She wanted to be with him in
every sense of the word. Intimate with him.

She bit her lip. "I thought we said we weren't
going to do this anymore."

"You said that. I didn't."

She was going to scream if she didn't get some
air. Sitting up, she pulled up her bra and dress. "Can
you zip me, please?" It was the least he could do
since he'd unzipped her.

Joshua frowned. "Yeah, but—"

Maddie made a strangled sound of frustration.
"Please?"

"Okay, okay." He zipped her, then eyed her war-
ily as she scooted to her seat and pushed open the
door. "What's with you?"

"Have you ever heard the expression 'Hotter than
a naked jalapeño pepper in June'?"

"Can't say that I have."

"Well, I feel like that jalepeño pepper right now!"
Maddie jumped to the ground, slammed the door behind her and fanned her face.

Joshua watched her in amazement. She looked as

out of control as he felt. For Pete's sake, he'd wanted to devour the woman. He'd mentally done an inventory of his feed supplies to keep from tearing through her nylons and begging her to let him in. He was still hard, still wanted her.

He had known he'd wanted her, but he'd had no clue how responsive she would be. He'd had no idea how her husky moan would feel like an intimate stroke. He'd had no idea she could possibly want him half as much as he wanted her.

Swearing, he breathed in deeply. His body felt tight, primed. For Maddie. Based on her little stroll in the cool night air, his body was not going to get what it wanted.

He squeezed the bridge of his nose. Hell, he was going to have to figure this out, but now was not the time. Right now, he had the brain power of a stud rearing to go. Which was zero.

He sighed and pushed open the car door to join her outside. The night air hit him like a slap. "Who needs a cold shower after this?"

Maddie pressed her lips together and gave a weak smile, but she didn't look at him. Her arms were crossed over her chest.

"Cat got your tongue?"

"No, you did."

His body responded immediately to the thought of her mouth, despite the cool temperature. "And I'd like it again," he said, and put his arm behind her on the side of the truck.

Maddie gave a soft groan and looked up at the stars. "I'm embarrassed."

He jerked his head to stare at her. "Why?"

"Because I lost it, just lost it. I was practically jumping you in your truck."

"I wish," he muttered, then shook his head. "I think you're confused."

"I won't argue with that."

"You weren't jumping me. I was jumping you."

She looked at him skeptically. "You look calmer than I feel."

"I have to. If I showed you how much I want you, I'm afraid it might scare you."

Her eyes widened, and she stared at him. "I've never been that out of control before. I don't think I like it."

"I did," he said without missing a beat.

She gave a shaky laugh, and the sound of it squeezed his heart. He took her chin in his hand and lowered his head. "Maddie, anytime you feel like losing control or jumping me, go right ahead."

Seven

"**B**ottle? What happened to—" Joshua's gaze dipped to her breasts as she sat on his sofa, and Maddie was struck with the memory of how he'd touched her last week.

"I switched to formula when I went back to work. No problem, for you, Studmuffin, huh? You just want your food," she said to Davey, and watched him smile around the bottle nipple. She sighed. "He's so gorgeous. He'll have to beat the girls off with a stick."

"Are you sure it won't be you beating the girls off with a stick?" Joshua asked with a lifted brow.

"Not if they're nice," she said sweetly.

Patrick patted Major, then walked up beside Joshua and crossed his arms over his chest. "He's not bad for a baby. He doesn't scream that much or anything."

Maddie chuckled. "Thanks. I wish I could take credit for his temperament, but I think it's most likely related to a mature digestive system."

"Oh, yeah?"

"That means he burps after she feeds him," Joshua said.

Patrick shrugged, and Maddie expected he might return to his room as he often did after dinner, but he stayed.

"Would you like to feed him?" she asked.

Patrick's face shifted to wariness. "I—uh—well—"

"You don't have to. I didn't know if you'd ever held and fed a baby before."

He shrugged again, his standard gesture. "Okay."

"Why don't you sit down beside me?" Maddie asked, and positioned David in Patrick's arms. "It probably won't take long. He's like a little Hoover." She patted David and smiled at Patrick. "You look like you've been doing this for years."

"He's fed some colts on occasion," Joshua said.

"That must be it." She noticed Patrick kept glancing at her, then looking away, as if he wanted to say something. She took a stab at what might be on his mind. "Have you talked to Amy since the dance?"

He nodded. "She talks to me at school."

Maddie nodded. "Do you say anything back?"

"Yeah," he said, then added, "when I can think of something."

Maddie lifted her eyebrows. "Does she make you a little nervous?"

"A little," he conceded, glancing quickly at his father. Fidgeting slightly, he cleared his throat. "When you were in high school, how did guys get you to go out with them?"

Maddie saw how much the question had cost him, and her heart went out to him. It made her chest tighten to think David might be asking her the same kind of question someday. "Well, they called me on the phone. They walked me to class and ate lunch with me. They asked me questions."

"What kind of questions?"

"Oh, what kind of music I liked, what movies I'd seen, what TV shows I watched. Those kind of things."

"I think he's done," Patrick said, since the bottle was empty and David was half-asleep.

"I think you're right." She lifted Davey to her shoulder and gently rubbed his back.

"Did it work?"

Confused, she looked at Patrick. "Did what work?"

"Asking questions and calling you on the phone. Did that make you go out with the guy?"

"Sometimes," she said. "It also depended on whether or not I thought he was cute."

"Oh," he said, his expression saying he didn't think he fell into the cute category. "Did flowers help?"

"Flowers always help, and they don't have to be roses," she told him, but didn't reveal the fact that she had never received flowers from a man. "Little presents help."

"Little?" Patrick's voice cracked in concern.

"Very little," she assured him. "A cassette of a favorite musical group. A key chain with my initial." Maddie was naming the gifts she would have liked to receive, but hadn't. She remembered again how Clyde had always been broke, and she smiled. "What works even more, though, is to listen to her. If you learn to listen well enough, you'll find out what she likes."

"Most women are more obscure than that," Joshua said cynically.

"Listening is a difficult skill for some men to master," she said right back at him.

"Tell her she's pretty. Tell her you like her hair, the way she smells and the way she smiles," Joshua said.

"That worked for you?" Patrick asked.

"Like a charm."

"But if it's a line," Maddie warned, not completely certain which Blackwell she was instructing, "then she may eventually find out, and she'll dump you. It needs to be the truth." She paused. "Tell her how she makes you feel."

"Like I'm gonna throw up?"

Joshua laughed and tossed Maddie a you-asked-for-it glance.

"Your good feelings," she said, looking down her nose at Joshua. "But that's after you go out with her. When you get to know her better, you might change your mind. That's what dating is for."

Patrick nodded. "Yeah, but where do I take her?"

"First date is ice cream," Joshua said. "Cheap and fast. You can't screw up ice cream."

Unable to resist some gentle ribbing, Maddie looked at him in amusement. "I'm surprised you remember back that far."

He gave her a swift glance full of heat and challenge. "Like riding a bike. You never forget."

Maddie felt her heart trip. Joshua reminded her of a bear who'd been hibernating. She'd mistaken him for half-dead, but now he was waking up. And he was hungry for her. She just wasn't sure what would be left of her if he consumed her.

She turned her attention back to Patrick. He was much safer. "This is going to sound hokey, but you would be surprised how much thoughtfulness and good manners will work."

Patrick looked as if he was processing all the information he'd received. "Did you dump many guys?"

"Enough," Maddie said wryly. "I think I attracted a lot of jerks back then." She laughed in memory. "There were some I should have dumped sooner than I did."

"Okay," Patrick said, and stood. "Thanks."

He started to leave the room, then turned around, a thoughtful expression on his face. "What was the best thing any guy ever gave you?"

"Besides David?" she asked, savoring the soft weight of her baby. She heard Joshua's swift intake of breath and knew what he must be thinking. "But you need to remember I'm twenty-seven, out of high school, and I would much prefer sharing the responsibility of raising a child.''

"Yeah, I know all about condoms."

"Yeah, well they can break," she muttered under her breath. "Two kinds of birth control are better than one, but you already know that. And I'm sure you already know it's more than bodies that are involved when people have sex, so you need to save it.'' She shot Joshua a quick glance and sensed his approval.

She smiled at Patrick. "My favorite gift from a guy was a song he wrote for me.'' She shook her head and sighed. "I've always been a sucker for a guy with a guitar.''

A few minutes later Joshua walked with her out to her car. The earlier rain had cleared, and the night air was once again cool. As soon as she tucked David into his car seat and closed the car door, Joshua pressed his chest and lower body against hers, gently trapping her against the car.

She told herself to ignore the way her heart jumped in her chest. "It might be kinda hard for me to get in and drive home.''

"You in a rush?" he asked, lowering his mouth to nuzzle her ear.

Maddie shuddered. "Not really. Just don't want to wear out my welcome.''

He skimmed his lips over her neck. "No chance.''

She tried to stifle a whimper, but didn't completely succeed.

He gave a low growl. "I love the little sounds you

make. It makes me wonder how you'd sound in bed."

A wicked, illicit thrill raced through her, but she was torn. "I don't know if that means I should shut up or not."

"Not," he told her. "Have I told you how pretty you are?"

Maddie melted, even though she knew it wasn't true.

He wove his fingers through her hair. "And I like your hair, the color, the way it feels, the way it moves."

Maddie closed her eyes. His hands felt good. His words felt wonderful. "Oh, Joshua."

He nuzzled her again. "I love the way you smell."

"Baby powder."

"It smells sexy on you."

She opened her eyes and laughed lightly. "You're crazy."

"Maybe." He lifted his finger to her lips. "I like the way you smile."

Not certain whether to laugh or cry, Maddie shook her head. "Very good, Joshua. Very good." She pushed hard at his chest and walked around to the driver's side of the car.

"What?" he demanded, following after her. "What?"

"Nice lines," she said. "They almost work like a charm."

"Aw, hell, Maddie, you knew I meant them."

"Well, here's one for you," she tossed back at him as she swung into her seat. "You make me feel like throwing up."

* * *

Joshua checked the window one more time and frowned.

"You don't see her?"

"No." This was the first Wednesday Maddie hadn't shown up with a meal in weeks and weeks. Although Joshua enjoyed her food, he wasn't nearly as concerned about the meal as he was about Maddie.

"You think we should call?" Patrick asked, revealing that he'd grown accustomed to her visits, too.

"Just a few more minutes," Joshua said, though his instinct was to go out looking for her. What if she'd found her way into his crazy neighbor's yard again, and this time the guy had decided to use his shotgun?

He heard a loud roar down his lane and felt a sliver of relief. That was Maddie's muffler. Major pawed at the door.

Patrick glanced at him and nodded. They both went to the door, ready to run down the steps to help her.

Maddie's car door opened, and a man got out with a pizza box. He ran up to the porch. His hair was long, he wore one tiny golden hoop earring, and he was dressed in jeans and a biker T-shirt. "Hey, I'm Ben, Maddie's brother. She can't come tonight. The baby's sick, so she asked me to bring you pizza. You're Joshua, right?"

Joshua nodded, seeing nothing of Maddie in the man until he looked into Ben's eyes. Same brown, same vitality. "Come in out of the rain and join us."

Ben hesitated a moment, then made a face at her car and shrugged. "Thanks. I think I will. There's two pizzas. Maddie told me to choose, so there's one super supreme and one pepperoni."

"You did good," Joshua said as they moved toward the kitchen. "Patrick will probably chew through the box."

"Da-ad," Patrick said in disgust, still surreptitiously staring at Ben.

Joshua grabbed some cans of soda from the refrigerator. "Bachelor china tonight, Patrick," he said.

Patrick pulled out paper plates and napkins, and Ben grinned in approval. "You mean there's another kind?"

"What's wrong with David?"

Ben shook his head. "Ear infection. She took him to the doctor and got some medicine, but he'll probably be screaming again tonight, poor kid."

Joshua winced. "Again?"

"Yep. She stayed up last night. I'd give her a break tonight, but I'm working the late shift at Tony's Bar." Ben took a bite of pizza and washed it down with soda. "She looks like hell."

An idea nudged at Joshua, and he let it ferment in his mind while he led the conversation in a different direction. "I don't know much about you, except you're the godfather," Joshua said, "and you were initially told Maddie had delivered quintuplets."

Ben chuckled darkly. "That's our Maddie. Keeps

us all on our toes." He gave Joshua an assessing glance. "I've gotten an earful about you."

Surprised, Joshua paused mid-bite. He swallowed. "Is that so?"

"Yep, she told me all about you and your son. Said Patrick was real bright. Great kid."

Patrick sat up straighter. "She did?" His voice broke, and he cleared his throat. "She did?" he repeated in a deeper tone.

"Yeah. And she's determined to stick out this meal thing even if it kills her."

A sliver of guilt stung him, and Joshua bit back an oath. "I've tried to get her to stop. It's not necessary."

"Forget it," Ben said. "She's made up her mind. She says you were there when she needed somebody and she won't forget it." Ben paused and flicked a mushroom off his pizza. "That's a new experience for Maddie, especially with a man. My dad traveled a lot when we were growing up, so he wasn't around much. And Clyde," Ben said in disgust, "was never around. That guy was more of a flake than Maddie. Talented, but he didn't deserve her."

He glanced at Joshua again, as if he were assessing him. "There's more to Maddie than meets the eye," he said in a soft, but firm voice.

Joshua took a second look at Ben again. He heard a subtle warning in his voice. The brother looking out for his sister. With the way Joshua felt about Maddie, perhaps someone should be looking out for her.

* * *

Late that night Joshua was restless and unable to sleep. He prowled through the den and kitchen, drank a glass of milk and ate a packaged cookie. Making a face as he ate the dry, tasteless cookie, he realized this was probably one of the reasons why he'd never gotten fat. His cooking sure wasn't anything to brag about, and he'd never possessed the knack for finding the good stuff at the grocery store. If he ate Maddie's cooking on a more regular basis, he'd bet he would be breaking the scale.

Joshua frowned. He had grown accustomed to seeing her once a week. He looked forward to it, sometimes even felt impatient about it. Feeling the burn of hunger inside him, he suspected the sensation had nothing to do with food and everything to do with Maddie.

He would like to think it was just sex, but something about Mad Maddie got under his skin and grabbed his heart. He wondered if she was walking the floor with David tonight. He remembered the loneliness of being the sole person responsible for a small child, and the idea of her fighting off the exhaustion during another long night nagged at him.

He rolled his shoulders and tried to dismiss the image, but it nagged and pulled and tugged. The same idea that had struck him during dinner nudged at him again.

"A crazy idea," he muttered, glancing at the kitchen clock which read 11:30 p.m. "Crazy."

Walking back to his room, he shoved on jeans, a shirt, socks and shoes, all the while muttering about "his freakin' crazy idea." He woke Patrick long enough to tell him where he would be, then took off in his truck.

With no traffic, he made the trip in thirty-five minutes. He was just going to check on her, he told himself, planning to keep his craziness to himself. If her town house was dark, he would turn around and go back home without even knocking on her door.

There was, however, a light.

He tapped lightly and waited, then tapped again. This was nuts, he thought, and was just turning to leave when the door opened.

With David propped on her shoulder and sucking his pacifier like there was no tomorrow, Maddie stared at Joshua for a full unblinking moment. He saw the wear and tear of the past twenty-four hours on her face. Shadows under her eyes, tousled hair, she wore a Betty Boop nightshirt. The sight of her self-consciously rubbing her damp cheeks and ducking her head turned him inside out. She was a mess, and he couldn't remember when a woman had affected him more.

"I heard you were having a rough night."

She nodded and sniffed. "You sure you want to join our sobfest?"

He bit back a grin and shrugged. "I didn't have anything better to do."

Maddie groaned in misery. "What about sleep?"

Already tried and couldn't, he thought wryly. "You gonna let me in?"

"Oh, sorry," she said as if the idea hadn't occurred to her. She stepped aside. "I wasn't expecting you."

"Or anyone else after midnight," Joshua murmured, and followed her into the den.

"Midnight?" She squinted her eyes at a porcelain clock on the fireplace mantel as she paced. "I hadn't noticed. Do you want coffee or milk or—"

"I want you to sit down," Joshua said, wondering if she was going to faint from exhaustion. He had the strongest urge to pick her up and carry her to bed, but he suspected she would protest.

Maddie glanced at him and shook her head. "No can do. Studmuffin here has got a killer earache, and walking him is his only relief. I can't bear to hear him cry anymore."

"Medicine?"

She continued to pace. "Yep. The doctor said it should kick in within twenty-four to forty-eight hours."

"You haven't asked why I came," Joshua said.

"No." Maddie gave a light laugh. "I guess I'm getting a little punchy."

"Ben said you had a rough night last night, too."

She nodded and focused on the pattern of her carpet.

"I remember how staying up with Patrick was rough sometimes. Makes for a helluva long night."

She nodded again.

"So I thought I'd take over for a while."

Maddie nodded yet again, continuing to pace.

Her lack of responsiveness made him uneasy. "Maddie, did you hear what I said?"

She looked up at him and blinked. "Gosh, I wish the room would stop moving."

For Pete's sake, the woman was practically swooning. He extended his arms. "Give me the little one, babe."

She frowned as if trying to understand. "Pardon?"

"I said, give me David, and you go to bed."

She closed her eyes. "No. Geez, I wish my equilibrium would get its act together. Don't worry. David'll settle down in a little while and—"

"You'll fall flat on your face if you don't get some sleep," Joshua said firmly. He gave a little flick of his fingers. "Give him to me."

Her gaze met his, and he could see that he had penetrated the thick fog of her weariness. He sensed she was finally seeing him for the first time this evening. A mixture of emotions played across her face. He watched her let go of her defenses just a little. Relief and trust smoothed her features. She trusted him. It was odd as hell, but her trust made him feel taller, stronger.

Even odder was the fact that underneath her weariness and all the other emotions, he knew she wanted him. It was more than a physical want, though it included desire. She wanted him for the man he was, inside and out. The wanting laid bare in her eyes rocked him.

"Just for an hour," she said, and handed David over to him, patting her baby and making sure his pacifier was secure. "Any longer wouldn't be fair. I'm not sure this is."

She looked at Joshua again and shook her head,

gratitude shining in her brown gaze. "You're an amazing man," she whispered, then rose on tiptoe and lightly kissed him. "Amazing. All I need is an hour. Wake me in an hour. Okay?"

"Sure."

Maddie awoke when the first sliver of sunlight peeked through the crack in her curtains. She lay still for a moment, sensing something wasn't quite right. She glanced quickly at David's bassinet and found it empty. The light dawned in more ways than one. She remembered Joshua and winced. He'd stayed all night. He must be exhausted.

Pushing off the covers, she scrambled downstairs and stopped dead at the entrance to her den. Joshua sat in the rocking chair, his feet spread apart on the floor, his large hands holding David securely against his chest and his head tipped forward.

David was sleeping. So was Joshua.

A rush of emotion squeezed her heart like a vice. Maddie took a deep breath. It almost hurt to look. To see a man hold David with such tenderness and care was the stuff of her dreams. She wanted David to have everything he needed, and as much as she tried, she could never be Daddy too. She'd just assumed she would have to go it alone, and though she knew Joshua wasn't in the market for a baby son, it was tempting to play with the magical thought for a moment.

What if Joshua fell in love with her and her baby and wanted to keep them both? What if...

Maddie shook herself and sighed. *Get a grip.* She couldn't blame herself for the momentary flight of fancy. For Pete's sake, when had any man inconvenienced himself for her well-being? Never, that she could remember. But she didn't want Joshua that way, she reminded herself. The reminder, however, was becoming more and more difficult for her to believe.

Stepping forward, she lightly pressed the back of her hand against David's forehead. Fever all gone. The tension inside her eased a little more, and she looked at Joshua again. His jaw was shadowed with a morning beard, his hair dark and tousled, his eyelashes, black spiky fans. His shirt was wrinkled, probably damp from baby drool.

Maddie had never seen a more beautiful man in her life. When had he changed, she wondered? Or had she changed? Suddenly his eyes opened, his gaze finding hers with such speed and intensity that she stopped breathing. An old, old feeling, its origins in her childhood, tightened her stomach.

She felt *caught*.

Eight

Maddie breathed again, then followed old instincts. When caught, talk. A lot.

"You didn't wake me after an hour," she chided Joshua, flustered, eager to break the spell and alleviate the "caught" feeling. "It was nice of you to give me a break, but I hate the idea of you spending the night in that chair. Here, let me change him and feed him." She reached for David and walked toward the kitchen. "If you'll give me just a minute, I'll get you some coffee."

"Maddie?" Joshua's voice carried to her as she rounded the corner.

She stopped. "Yes?"

"You can skip the coffee. I'll leave in a minute or two."

His words spurred her into action again. "No, no,

no." As David gummed her shoulder, Maddie pulled a bottle from the refrigerator and put it in the microwave to knock the chill off. After placing David in his high chair, she pulled out his antibiotic liquid. "Let me at least get you some coffee. If you can wait a little longer, I can fix you some breakfast and—"

"Hey." Joshua came up behind her. "Why the tizzy?"

Maddie paused as she poured the medicine into the infant spoon. Her heart was racing. Her mind was in turmoil. She felt all out of control. "Nobody's ever really been there for me when I needed help. Well, except for Emily and Jenna Jean, and sometimes Ben."

She gave David his medicine and watched him make a face. "Good boy," she murmured, shaking his formula and testing the temperature before she popped it in his mouth.

She finally looked up at Joshua. "I feel awkward. It means a lot to me, what you did last night—"

Joshua shrugged. "It wasn't a big deal."

"Yes, it was," she said emphatically. "It was a big deal to me, and I don't know how to thank you."

His gaze shifted with a hint of underlying sexuality. Maddie glanced down at her Betty Boop nightshirt and was certain she'd misread him.

"You're feeling grateful?"

"Yes."

"How grateful?" he asked in a deep, rumbly voice that did wicked things to her nerve endings. He moved closer.

Maddie swallowed, then gave a short laugh. Someone needed to set this man straight. "I'm presently wearing a five-year-old nightshirt, feeding a baby, and I haven't checked the mirror, but I'm pretty sure my hair is sticking out in every possible direction on the compass. You couldn't possibly want me at this moment." Despite her protest she saw desire in his eyes. "Not unless you're blind."

He shook his head. "Twenty-twenty vision."

Perfect. Why didn't that surprise her? "Or you're crazy."

He gave a short laugh of his own and dipped his mouth to her neck. "Now that is possible."

Maddie closed her eyes against a flood of sensations. "You can't want me. You can't. It's just not—"

His hand curved around her hip and stopped her words. "I can," he told her, tugging her nightshirt up her thighs and sliding his fingers along her bare skin. He opened his mouth and gently sucked at the skin on her throat. "And I do."

Maddie felt like a toaster on broil. She bit back a moan when his fingers skimmed higher. Her nipples began to tingle and she had to fight the urge to rub her thighs together. "Joshua," she said.

"The question is do you want me?"

"Oh, help."

David whimpered, and Maddie opened her eyes. Muttering at herself, she stared at Joshua in accusation. "You're trying to wreck me."

"Think so?" His eyes were smoky gray, and his voice had a thigh-melting quality to it.

Maddie lifted her chin, seeing trouble in her future. "Yes, and you better stop it."

"Oh, yeah?"

"Yeah," she said, putting an extra note of belligerence in her voice.

"Turnabout's fair play. You wreck me, I wreck you. And now that I've sat up with David all night, I'd say you owe me."

Maddie's mouth went dry. She told herself it was shock and not excitement. He couldn't possibly mean— He didn't really expect her to show her gratitude in a sexual manner. A wicked voice inside her told her it would be the most enjoyable thank-you she'd delivered.

"Ice cream," Joshua said.

Completely befuddled, she stared at him. "Ice cream?"

"Friday night." He gave her a mock innocent look. "Can't go wrong with ice cream."

And Maddie realized she'd been deceived. Joshua was not a stick-in-the-mud. He was only disguised as one. He was, in fact, a wolf.

They didn't get the ice cream until later Friday night because Joshua had needed to take care of some horse business. By the time they arrived at the ice cream shop, it was mobbed, so they bought cartons and took them to Maddie's house.

Joshua was in a crazed mood. He hadn't felt like this in years. If he didn't have Maddie Palmer, he feared he was going to have to be committed. He felt like the Tasmanian Devil, and he was fighting the urge to take her on the kitchen table.

"Who did you say is taking care of David?" he asked, as she pulled chocolate, strawberry and butterscotch syrup out of the cupboard.

"My friend, Jenna Jean. She fussed at me for not calling her one of the nights he was sick, but I didn't even think of it. She's assistant DA," she told Joshua, "and she can tear a strip off you during an argument, so I just told her she could keep David another time." She pulled a can of whipped cream from the refrigerator and grinned. "I picked tonight."

Joshua looked from the whipped cream to Maddie and back to the whipped cream. In his wicked mind, wicked possibilities abounded. He cleared his throat. "Do you like a little ice cream with your toppings?"

Her grin grew and she slit her eyes at him. "A little ice cream. Are you a purist?"

He didn't feel the least bit pure around her. "I take some chocolate syrup on top every now and then."

She put Oreo cookies, sprinkles and bananas on the table. "It sounds like you might need to expand your tastes."

"I'm trying," Joshua muttered, watching her flit around the kitchen.

She played spoons for a few seconds, then put them on the table next to the bowls. She lifted her hand over the assortment of toppings. "Well, what's your pleasure?"

"Tough to choose," he said.

"Then maybe I can help," she suggested, and

opened the small cartons. "You picked the lime sherbet. That limits the options. Even I don't put chocolate and lime together. But strawberry syrup? Bananas?"

She scooped the ice cream, poured the syrup and sliced half a banana. "Whipped cream?" she asked.

Joshua was having a tough time keeping his brain from sinking below his belt. "Is it good?"

She frowned, then glanced at the can. "It's not expired." She squirted a dot on her finger and licked it. "Tastes good to me." She waited a moment and shrugged. "You wanna try it?"

"Yeah," Joshua said.

She squirted more on her finger and lifted it presumably for him to swipe with his own finger. Instead, Joshua closed his hand around her wrist and lifted her finger to his mouth. He felt her jolt of surprise when he licked the cream...and her finger.

She jerked her hand away and looked down her nose at him. "That was tricky."

"If you would show a little pity," he said, emphasizing the word, "I wouldn't have to resort to such measures."

She stared at him for three seconds before he saw the beginning of a slow burn. "Pity?"

"Yeah." He scooted the bowl toward him and took a spoonful. "You kiss me, and just when I start to get out of control, you stop." He swallowed another bite and hoped it would cool the heat that seemed to burn inside him all the time lately. "You get close and then you move away. I wouldn't have thought you'd be such a tease, Maddie."

"Tease!" Looking hot enough to fry an egg on her body, she shook the can of whipped cream at him.

Joshua snickered. "Be careful where you point that. I was just kidding," he said, then added, "kinda."

"Kinda!" She pressed the nozzle on the whipped cream and sprayed him with it. Not just his hand or even his face, but his shirt. A dollop of it fell to his jeans.

Incredulous, Joshua looked at her. She appeared almost as appalled as he was.

"Oops." She gave a weak smile and put the can down. "Didn't mean to get your shirt."

Joshua shook his head. "You have a napkin?"

"Oh, sure. Just a second." She fluttered into action, pulling several from the counter and rushing to his side. She swiped at his shirt several times, then glanced down at his thigh.

Her brown-eyed gaze inched up his body and Joshua felt it, like he would have a series of open-mouth kisses on his bare skin. When she finally met his gaze, he could see bewilderment and arousal warring in her eyes.

She wore a sleeveless peach-colored dress that suited her personality. It was a warm evening, and her legs were bare except for a gold chain with hearts around her ankle and the sandals on her pretty feet. The swinging hem of her dress and the winking gold chain, along with her mischievous brown eyes and catch-me-if-you-can smile taunted the hell out of him.

Joshua gave in to one of the urges he'd been fighting all night. Sliding his hand just above her knee, he rubbed the naked silky skin of her shapely leg.

Maddie went still.

Her heart tripping over itself, she took a careful breath. There was something different about Joshua tonight. He seemed as if all he would need was a little push and he would be out of control.

The idea excited and unnerved her, and she wasn't totally certain how she wanted to respond. She did know, however, that she liked the way he looked at her, as if she were ice cream and he could eat her with a spoon. She liked the way his voice felt in her mind and sensitive places. She liked his hand on her leg way too much for uncertainty.

She cleared her throat. "The-uh-ice cream's melting."

He slid his fingers a little higher, and her chest tightened.

"Joshua," she managed, but the sound wasn't much of a protest.

"Maddie," he returned, his gaze knocking down her resistance. "When are you gonna put me out of my misery?"

Maddie sighed and slid her hand over his jaw. She liked the slightly raspy feel of his five o'clock shadow. Too much. "Joshua, you don't want to get involved with me."

He drew her between his legs so that she was flush against him. "I'm already involved."

"You are?"

He gave a slow nod and slid one of his legs between hers. "Yeah, and you are, too. Come closer, babe." He brushed his mouth over hers.

She felt herself sinking. Into his gaze, into his kiss, into him.

He pulled her down, making it so easy for her to slide her leg around and straddle him. "You should get involved with a different kind of woman," she warned him, and kissed him. "A woman who doesn't leave pacifiers in your driveway. Or get a flat tire you think you need to change."

She nuzzled his throat as he pushed her skirt up. "You should get involved with a woman who understands about studs and mares and settling and—"

"Maddie, I want you." He took her mouth, his tongue making love to hers.

It was a sensual, carnal kiss that made her heart tighten and her breath grow scarce. He slid his fingers between her legs to where she was moist and hot. Maddie gasped and ducked her head. "I'm trying to warn you."

He tipped her head upward and eased his finger inside her. "You feel so good."

She instinctively tightened. She wanted him. Oh, how she wanted him. "We're not going to make it to the bedroom, are we?" she whispered.

Joshua sucked at her bottom lip and gave a swift tug at her panties. There was a quick shredding sound. "Not the first time," Joshua said.

Maddie unzipped his jeans and freed his hardened masculinity.

"That's right. Touch me," he urged, still snatching kisses, still caressing her intimately.

She moaned and stroked him. He was full with need, already moist with desire.

His rough sound of fascination and approval urged her on. She knew he was watching her. His arousal stirring hers, she rolled her forefinger over him, then lifted his honey to her mouth.

He closed his eyes as if in pain. "Oh, Maddie. Where have you been— Where—" Breaking off, he dug into his pocket and pulled out a plastic packet.

She lost a little more of her heart when she saw that he'd come prepared. Considerate, solid, sexy.

He kissed her again, and the room felt as if it turned upside down. A moment passed, then another, and he was lifting her, positioning her over him. Then he gently guided her down until he filled her.

They stared at each other, joined intimately. Passion, desire, wonder. She undulated and watched him shudder. The shudder echoed inside her.

"Oh, lady." He wrapped his hands around her bottom and moved her in rhythm.

The pleasure grabbed and pulled at her. He looked at her as if she were the most beautiful woman in the world. She rode him, feeling his strength and need swell inside her.

He said her name, and a soft sound bubbled from her throat. He looked at her as if she were the only one who could satisfy him.

Maddie followed his faster rhythm, feeling the coil of sensation tighten inside her. Spinning higher and higher, she held tightly to him, never taking her gaze from his face.

Some part of her noticed he never took his gaze

from her, either, and that he held her as tightly as she held him. He chanted her name again and again, but his eyes told her stories she was afraid to believe. His eyes told her this was more than want and need for him. His eyes told her that he loved her. That was when Maddie went over the edge. And Joshua tumbled after her.

The aftershocks rocked through them both, and they clung to each other, hearts pounding, breathing hard. He nudged her mouth up to his and kissed her gently, tenderly.

Then he looked at her and shook his head. "Oh, Maddie, heaven help me," he muttered in a husky voice. "I want you again."

She laughed weakly, laying her head on his shoulder. "Heaven help me. I want you again, too."

He squeezed her to him, and though he was still inside her, she knew what he was feeling. That close wasn't close enough. "Let's go upstairs."

She nodded. "Can you walk?"

His lips tilted into an affectionate grin. "Yeah."

"Show-off," she said, her legs still feeling like gelatin.

"It's okay," he said, shifting slightly, then standing. "I'll walk both of us."

"There's something very unfair about this." She tried to frown, but couldn't. She was too giddy.

He arched a dark eyebrow. "Unfair?"

"Yeah," she said, then impulsively picked up the can of whipped cream. "Let's see if I can improve the odds."

An hour and a half later, Joshua lay sprawled on

her bed, trying to catch his breath. The can of whipped cream was empty. It had become an erotic battle of wills to see who would get the last dollop. Maddie had won. Just barely.

He stared down at her. She was a wholly feminine mess of tousled hair, bare skin, swollen lips from kissing and long lean limbs wrapped around him. She smelled like whipped cream and sex, and if he dwelled on that thought for longer than thirty seconds, then he would take her again.

At the moment her eyes were closed, and she breathed deeply, evenly. He might have thought she was sleeping except for the slight movement of her hand on his chest, back and forth, stroking gently. The tenderness in the gesture grabbed at his gut and twisted.

The way she affected him was amazing. When she made love with him, she held nothing back. Joshua had never experienced a woman giving to him so completely. Maddie wasn't one to sit back and be taken. She would do her share of the taking, too. The experience filled him with emotion. And questions.

Her eyes opened, and she met his gaze wordlessly.

"I have a personal question," he said.

"Okay. Ask."

"This man you were involved with for a long time…"

She nodded. "Clyde."

"He was away most of the time. I wondered if you made love with him like you did with me."

Her eyes widened, and she shifted slightly. "That is personal. Do you mean with whipped cream?"

He shrugged. "No. I mean with—" He searched for the right word. "With the same intensity."

She gave him a puzzled look. "Why do you ask?"

"If you did, then the guy probably didn't stay around much because he was afraid he'd die of cardiac arrest."

Maddie burst out laughing. "Oh, I don't think so." She shook her head at him, then her face grew more serious. "To answer your question, no, it's never been this intense for me." She paused, and her eyes darkened with a hint of uncertainty. "Too much?"

He shook his head. "No. Not at all."

He kissed her and felt her turn to liquid, and he wanted her again. "We just had each other," he said in disbelief.

She sighed. "I know, and we've got to stop." Regret muted her voice. "I need to go get David. I don't want to terrify Jenna Jean this first time alone with him."

He fought disappointment and chuckled to himself. He was nuts. He gave her a quick kiss. "Let me drive you."

Surprise and pleasure softened her face. "Thank you. That would be very nice."

At first glance Jenna Jean Anderson was the antithesis of Maddie. Jenna had a cool, pulled-together image. Her brunette hair was neatly pulled back at the nape of her neck, and even in her jeans and blouse, she looked crisp and in control.

She probably wouldn't be caught dead in Maddie's dream catcher earrings, and she didn't seem the nurturing type. Maddie was warm and wild. Jenna was cool and rational.

Joshua didn't understand the close association between the two until Maddie mentioned how long they had been friends. "Jenna Jean and I have known each other since I was six and she was seven."

Jenna lifted a dark eyebrow. "I go by Jenna," she said to Joshua, then looked at Maddie. "Still pushing the age factor, I see."

Maddie grinned. "Age before beauty. How did Davey do?"

Jenna's face softened slightly. "David was divine. We discussed one of my cases and he agrees with my plans to ask for the maximum on a repeat DWI. I think he's gifted," Jenna continued. "I'm not kidding. He seemed as if he was listening to every single word. He was smiling and talking back to me."

Maddie slid a quick, sly glance to Joshua. "Did he offer any other suggestions?"

"No, but he's very discriminating. He yawned when I told him about my boss."

"Everybody yawns when you talk about your boss," Maddie said. "I take it he's asleep right now?"

"In my bedroom in the portable crib you brought."

"Okay," Maddie said, walking toward the hallway. "Back in a minute."

Jenna immediately turned to Joshua with an assessing glance. "So you're the man who helped deliver David?"

Joshua nodded. "I did."

"Maddie mentioned you run a horse farm. That can be a little risky, can't it?"

"It can be, depending how you run your business," he said, wondering where she was heading with her questions.

She casually gestured toward the sofa, but Joshua would swear she was weighing his every move. "And what about yours?" she asked.

"Are you asking if I'm solvent?"

She didn't miss a beat. "Not really, but that's an interesting question if you'd like to answer it."

He sat down and began to get a hint of her courtroom tactics. "I'm solvent."

Jenna nodded solemnly. "Maddie also mentioned you have a teenage son. Do you like children?"

He shrugged. "I like kids, some more than others."

She considered that, then folded her hands in front of her. "I suppose that's fair." She paused again, thinking. Her lips twitched. "Maddie has always had a—" she searched for the word "talent for—"

"Unfortunate experiences with authority figures," Joshua finished for her. "Or trouble."

"She's not a troublemaker," Jenna insisted, and Joshua liked her for defending Maddie. "She just gets caught. People closely associated with her develop a tolerance for—"

"Messes," Joshua finished again.

Jenna nodded. "Yes. Do you think of yourself as a flexible type of individual?"

He could have been offended if he didn't understand the basis for her questions. "Flexible to a point.

I've got my limits. But, Jenna, are you sure we don't need a couple of witnesses and a Bible for this discussion?''

She struggled with a smile because she liked being in control, and he wasn't letting her. ''I hope you're smarter than Clyde was. He didn't know what he had. Maddie's changed,'' Jenna continued. ''She's not going to settle anymore.''

Settle for what? he wanted to ask, but Maddie breezed back into the room. And Joshua was left with a question that lingered.

Nine

"Sighing, swooning," Jenna Jean said as she, Maddie, and Emily sat by Emily's mother's swimming pool. "You're disgusting."

"I know," Maddie agreed with a smile she knew was ridiculously huge. Nothing could dispel her great mood. "You ought to try a little sighing and swooning, yourself, Jenna Jean." Turning down the volume on the CD boom box, Maddie gave an exaggerated sigh and made a thumping motion with her hand over her heart. "Besides, I've got a good reason for it, and you've met him."

"Told you she was loopy. He's better than Clyde, though, God rest his soul," Jenna Jean conceded.

Emily rubbed in sunscreen and frowned at the clouds. "When do I get to meet him?"

"I don't know. Joshua is out of town this weekend

for some kind of Horse Breeder's Association meeting. Since you and Beau don't get to town very often..."

Emily sipped her lemonade. "We'll have to plan something then. With their mutual interest in horses, I think Joshua and Beau would get along."

Jenna Jean sat up and laughed. "Who would have thought our Emily would marry a cowboy?"

"Well," Emily said with a sly expression, "if I couldn't be a cowboy, marrying one was the next best thing." She glanced at Maddie. "I remember being afraid Maddie would turn into a rock groupie."

Maddie made a face. "I never liked the idea of being one of many. I wanted to be one, period. Maybe that's why Joshua has turned my head. He's different. He doesn't look at me and think 'temporary fling.' He's not that kind of man, and he wants me." He wants me. The notion still knocked her off-kilter.

The whole subject made her nervous and excited, unable to sit still. She stood and began to pace. "He's too good to be true. It's like one of those 'find what's wrong with this picture' exercises we did when we were kids. I keep looking for reasons why it won't work, and he keeps eliminating them. He calls me regularly," she said in amazement, because it was a novel experience for her.

Maddie shook her head and thought of David and how much she had changed over the last year. "I just don't want to mess up this time." For all her supposed swooning and sighing, she wrestled with an ever present fear. "I don't want to be foolish."

"You won't," Jenna Jean said to her. "You've

got your head on straight, and I think Joshua Blackwell knows he has found one in a million.''

"If he makes you happy, that's what matters,'' Emily said.

"But if he treats you bad,'' Jenna Jean began, and stood.

"We'll get him,'' Emily and Jenna Jean finished together.

Jenna Jean smiled. "Now are you two going to be sun princesses all day or are you going to get wet? Last one in the pool is a rotten egg.''

"Looks like a sky full of diamonds,'' Maddie said as she lay on the blanket with Joshua. They'd gone out to dinner, and since it was such a warm, clear night, he'd brought her up to his hill. She could feel his warm gaze on her.

"Who has given you diamonds?''

Maddie's heart jumped, but she laughed to cover it. "More likely cubic zirconia or Austrian crystal.''

"Did you miss the rocks?''

He took her hand, and she looked at him. "Diamonds?'' she asked, and he nodded. Maddie thought about it. "No,''she said, "and yes.''

"Uh-huh,'' he said, looking at her as if she made no sense at all.

Maddie propped herself up on her elbow. "In itself I know the dollar figure on a gift is unimportant. I think it's more the symbolism behind it— that somebody would think I'm that important.'' She searched his gaze. "Does that make any sense?''

"I think so. What kind of presents did Clyde give you?"

Maddie chuckled again. "You mean when he remembered."

Joshua narrowed his eyes.

Maddie had to think. Clyde had been forgetful. "He gave me a lot of CDs that he liked, several demo tapes, some silver earrings from Mexico." She laughed in recollection. "He brought me peanut brittle once, but he ended up eating it. I never did like peanut brittle," she mused, then looked at Joshua and tried to read his expression. "What are you thinking? Say it out loud."

"Clyde sounds like he was a self-absorbed son-ovabitch."

Maddie nodded and smiled. "Yep, I guess he was."

"Then why did you stay with him so long?"

Maddie sighed, sat up and drew her legs to her chest. "I don't know. It was easier to stay with him than break it off. I think we were more of a habit for each other, and there was some security in that. People have all kinds of habits. Like you," she said, more than willing to turn the conversation away from herself.

"Me?"

"Sure. Why haven't you gotten involved with a woman for so many years?"

He shrugged. "I've been busy."

Maddie rolled her eyes. "Lame, lame, lame."

He wrapped his hand around her wrist and pulled her against his chest in a swift, economical motion.

"Who are you calling lame?" he asked, his eyes playfully warning, yet sexually intense.

Maddie jutted out her chin. "You."

"I've been busy."

"You've been wearing blinders," Maddie told him, forcing herself to concentrate as he slid his hands up the sides of her breasts. "You've cut yourself off from the female gender."

He shifted his pelvis so that she could feel his hardness against her. "Maybe I just didn't come across anyone who tripped my trigger."

She laughed breathlessly. "That's what you call it? Your trigger."

"Yeah," he said, skimming his hands down to her hips. "So what are you gonna do about it?"

It was one sexy, irresistible dare, and he made her want so much she felt like screaming. She shook her head and make a tsking sound. "I never would have thought you would be the type to go for this kind of outdoor activity."

His eyes darkened dangerously. "Is that so?" He rolled over so that she was beneath him. "And what type am I?"

Oops. Her stomach took a dip when he pressed his open mouth against her throat. "Type?" she repeated, hedging. She couldn't tell him what she'd really thought of him.

"*Yeah.* You think I'm the kind who draws the shades, turns out the light and makes love in the bed in the dark."

"Thought," she corrected. "What are you doing to my shorts?"

"Helping," he murmured, "to educate you about what kind of man I am."

The cool night air whispered over her skin, then his warm hands caressed her. Her heart raced, and she trembled. "I thought you'd already done that."

"Oh, baby, I've just gotten started with you."

A warning or a promise? An illicit thrill ran through her as he kissed her. He wasn't actually going to take her on this hill among the stars, was he? Maddie remembered the whipped cream and groaned.

He slipped one of his hands up her shirt and rubbed her already stiff nipple. "I think it's about time I tripped your trigger," Joshua said as he began to make a slow, breathtaking journey down her body with his mouth.

No one had ever made her feel this wanted. The feeling turned her to liquid. How did he do this to her? Fighting for a shred of sanity, Maddie joked, "Last time I looked, I didn't have a trigger."

He swirled his tongue around her belly button, and she shuddered. "Then I'll make you see stars," he promised, lowering his mouth again, this time between her thighs to the aching, moist heart of her. "I'll make you see stars inside."

Joshua's hands held her hips, and his tongue made magic. But it was his intimate words, his sounds of approval, need and want that sent her over and over again. And even when Maddie closed her eyes, she saw stars.

When he took her home that night, Maddie felt very vulnerable to him. It scared her, because she felt as if she would do anything for him. That could be dangerous. Then she looked at him, though, and saw his solid strength stamped across his features, across his body. He was a kind man, she reminded herself. A good man, who wouldn't take advantage of her. She could trust him.

Joshua came inside with her and talked with Ben for a few moments while she checked on David. Ben had taken care of David for the evening, insisting her son needed regular exposure to male influence, so he wouldn't end up thinking like a woman.

At another time she would have argued with him, but tonight she was in a daze. When she walked downstairs, Ben was gone.

"He needed to get to his job," Joshua said.

Maddie nodded. "Bouncing at the bar. Well, my brother did a pretty good job. David's diaper isn't on backward or anything."

Joshua chuckled, then pulled her to him. "You're an incredible woman, Maddie. I've never met anyone like you."

"Is that good or bad?"

"Good," he said. "Very good."

Swallowing a lump in her throat, Maddie took her heart in her hand. "I feel the same way about you. I've never met a man like you, who makes me—" She looked into his eyes. "Makes me feel like this." And hope. And believe.

"You're so honest and generous." He shook his head as if he couldn't believe she existed. "Most women want something back," he said. "Marriage or money. They want ownership. But you—'' He cupped his hand under her jaw. ''You understand. You don't have to have a man on a leash to know you've got him how it counts.''

An unsettling sensation fluttered in her stomach. ''On a leash?''

''Yeah. You're an incredibly rare woman,'' he told her, ''because you don't have to have marriage.''

Oh, yes I do. I thought you knew that. She felt as if she were on an elevator and the cable had just been cut. She couldn't have said a word if she'd had one in her head. Joshua continued to talk, but she didn't hear him.

She had been fooled again. Her stomach twisted violently. She had fooled herself again. Why had she been so stupid? Why had she thought he would see her differently than any other man? Just because he was solid and dependable? Just because he had helped deliver her baby, change a flat tire and relieved her that night David had been sick?

God, she hurt. She'd never hurt like this for a man. With Clyde she'd never really trusted him enough to put her hope in the future. But she'd allowed herself to hope with Joshua. She had been so totally and incredibly foolish. He was just like other men, except in a different wrapping.

He was still touching her, but she was so physically frozen she couldn't feel it. She watched his mouth form words. He lowered his head to hers as if he was going to kiss her and she flinched.

He looked at her quizzically. ''You okay?''

She blinked away the fog and nodded. A lie.

He kissed her lightly. "See you Wednesday."

No. She meant to shake her head, but she moved it in a circle. *The meals.* Her mind raced. What would she do about the meals?

"G'night, babe," he said, then walked out the door.

As the door clicked shut, she whispered, "Goodbye, Joshua."

She felt so stupid and angry she needed to break something. "I'm not going to cry," she told herself in a shaky voice. "I'm not going to cry."

Staring down at her feet, she willed them to move and headed for the kitchen, still chanting, "I'm not going to cry."

She opened the cupboard and pulled out a jelly glass and threw it hard into the sink. "He's not worth it."

Such crazy dreams she'd had. So crazy she wouldn't even share them with anyone. She pulled out another jelly glass and looked at it.

"My heart isn't broken."

Liar.

Her stomach twisted. Her throat was so tight her voice was hoarse. "It's only bruised," she insisted, and smashed the glass into the sink.

She looked for another jelly glass, but paused, her mind flying in a million directions. "Why did I do this to myself?"

She felt as if her chest was in a vise. Her eyes burned. "I'm not going to cry," she said around the huge lump in her throat. But her cheeks were wet from tears. Another lie. Maddie's shoulders sank. A deep, aching disappointment shuddered through her. Disappointment in herself and Joshua. No more lies, she thought, wiping her cheeks and letting the tears flow. She'd told herself too many.

Joshua looked at the chicken parmesan and frowned. The chicken was good, but he hadn't talked to Maddie in three days. He was beginning to wonder if she was avoiding him.

"When did you say she came?" he asked Patrick again.

Patrick swallowed a bite. "I'd just gotten home from school. She wasn't here but a minute." He took a gulp of milk. "Said she was in a big hurry." He stuffed half a roll in his mouth.

Joshua felt doubt tugging at him. Doubt and disappointment. "Did she say anything else?"

Patrick's eyebrows furrowed in concentration, and he shook his head. Then he stopped abruptly, his face clearing. "Oh, yeah."

Joshua felt a trickle of relief and he rolled his shoulders. A message for him, he thought. An explanation about where she'd been. A promise to call.

Patrick grinned and talked around a bite of chicken. "She said to put the Jell-O in the fridge."

Joshua tried calling her twice a day for the next several days. If his schedule hadn't been so packed and he hadn't been working from dawn to dusk, he would have driven into town to see her. As it was, he barely had time to eat.

Since he'd first made love to Maddie, he'd dreamed every night, all night. One of those crazy, inexplicable things, he'd told himself. Probably related to hormones. Lately when he slept, he only had snatches of dreams. They didn't last the whole night. He couldn't explain the change. He sure as hell didn't have the time or energy to try.

Lack of energy or time, however, didn't stop him from wondering what was going on with Maddie. By Wednesday he decided to devote the afternoon and evening to paperwork so he wouldn't miss her.

He heard the buzz of her muffler long before she pulled in front of his house. At the sound of her cutting her engine, Joshua opened the door to offer his help, but she was already moving quickly toward his front porch. Her hair bounced with her movements. Her skirt swished against her legs. Her vitality was contagious. He noticed a Band-Aid on her ankle and wondered what she'd bumped into. At first glance she made his heart pound faster.

At second glance when her gaze briefly met his and her step faltered as if she wasn't pleased to see him, he immediately knew something was wrong.

"Hi. Sunny today, isn't it?" she said as she flitted past him. "I brought a meat 'n' potatoes meal tonight. Pepper steak, mashed potatoes and gravy, and green beans. Hope you and Patrick enjoy it. Speaking of Patrick, where is he?"

Following her into the kitchen, Joshua frowned. "He stayed after school for a special computer class. Where have—"

"Computer," Maddie repeated brightly. A little too brightly, he thought. "That's great. I bet he's good with computers."

Joshua nodded. "Yes, but—"

"I put the pudding in the fridge. Sorry I've gotta run, but I need to pick up Davey at the sitter," she said as she practically raced for the door. "It was nice seeing—"

Just as she reached for the door, he stepped in front of her and blocked her. He felt like a stud trying to corral a jittery female. "What's going on?"

She met his gaze again briefly, then glanced away and shrugged. "It's a busy day. I need to pick up Davey from the sitter."

"Have you gotten my telephone messages?"

She crossed her arms over her chest and took a deep breath. She seemed to be studying the toe of her shoe. "Yes."

He wondered ironically where the chatterbox had gone. "Did you think about returning my calls?"

She made a restless move with her arms. "Yes."

Lord, he felt like he was pulling teeth. "Any particular reason you didn't?"

She nodded. "Yes."

Joshua waited in silence, but she said nothing. He ground his teeth together. "Would you like to share it with me?"

She paused as if she wasn't at all certain she wanted to share anything with him, and her hesitation got under his skin. He swore under his breath. "Okay, Maddie, quit playing chicken," he said, and watched her head snap upward. He pulled her against him and struggled with an urge to kiss the resistance out of her. "Tell me what the hell is going on. The last time I was with you we were as close as two

people can get. The last time we were together we
made love.''

Her brown gaze finally met his, defiant, yet disappointed in a way that made his gut sink. "I
screwed up," she said flatly. "I thought you and I
wanted the same thing, but I was wrong. I can't be
with you that way anymore.''

Ten

Joshua thought he would have recovered more quickly if she'd kicked him in the groin. This sharp pain, however, was much higher. He stared at her. "What in hell are you talking about?"

"Exactly what I said," she told him, and wiggled as if she was trying to get away from him.

Joshua instinctively tightened his hands. "What is this stuff about not wanting the same thing?"

She took a deep breath. "We don't. I want a more permanent relationship. I thought you did, too, but you don't. My fault," she said quickly in a soft voice. "I'm not blaming you. I'm not trying to trick you or change you, but I want more than I've had in the past." She shook her head. "I can't settle for what I had before. I have someone else to think about now. Davey."

Settle. Now he knew what Jenna Jean had meant. He bit back a silent oath.

She gave a shaky, terrible attempt at a smile and made a choking sound he'd bet she intended as a laugh. "And call me crazy, but maybe there's somebody out there who will look at me and see more than a good time."

Everything inside him roared in protest. "You're more than a good—"

She held up a hand and shook her head. "Joshua, this isn't necessary. I know you're trying to be kind, but I don't need your reassurance. I don't blame you. I understand what you want. I simply can't give it, and this whole thing is embarrassing for me, so I'd just like to go." She looked away from him and waited a few seconds. "Please."

He couldn't let her go. His hands, his body, his mind would not let her go. It was more than unacceptable. It was untenable. He shook his head, rejecting everything she'd said. "No. I—"

The door whooshed open into Maddie, pushing both of them backward. He heard Patrick call out, "I'm home!"

Maddie used the moment to pry Joshua's fingers from her arms and step away from him. He watched her force a smile for his son and greet him. "I've gotta run. I'll see you two next week. Take care, now."

She whirled through the open doorway and ran down the steps. She started her engine, her muffler scaring the birds out of the trees. Fighting the urge to stop her, Joshua clenched his fists and knew with sinking certainty that he had just let the best thing that had happened to him slip right through his fingers.

"Dad. Hey, Dad," Patrick said for the third time. "What's with you and Maddie? I thought you and she were—"

Tearing his gaze from the exhaust Maddie's car had left in its wake, Joshua looked at Patrick and saw the questions all over his son's face. He sighed. "I thought we were, too," he muttered, and closed the door behind them.

"So what happened? Did you dump her or something?" Patrick asked as he followed Joshua into the kitchen.

The irony was enough to make him choke. Joshua shook his head. "No. She dumped me."

Patrick's eyes rounded. "No way!"

His chest hurt, and he felt a gnawing ache he was determined to categorize as hunger for dinner. "Yes. She dumped me."

"Geez, Dad. What did you do? Maddie's so cool. She would have to be really ticked off to dump you, wouldn't she?"

The truth was painfully clear to Joshua. Maddie had opened her heart to him and let him in. She had been warm and willing and loving in a way no one had ever been to him.

Maddie had not been the one to mess up.

"I screwed up," he said to Patrick. It was simple. He'd rolled the dice and lost, and Joshua fought the certain, but sickening feeling that this loss could have a significant impact on the rest of his life.

* * *

Joshua's dreams faded completely away. There wasn't even a glimmer of any nocturnal vision that graced him. His nights returned to drab, endless black deserts. It was like a winter that wouldn't end. He dreaded going to bed at night and hated the way he felt when he woke in the morning.

He told himself there were advantages to getting back his precious peace and quiet. He wasn't changing tires in the rain. He wasn't delivering pacifiers to single mothers. He wasn't losing sleep while he rocked a fretful baby with an ear infection. It had been weeks since the birds in his trees had exhibited signs of nervous breakdowns from the sound of Maddie's muffler, because she'd delivered the last few meals via her brother. Major didn't bark his head off when she came within earshot.

Everything was quieter. It was an improvement, he insisted. He liked it better this way. He liked his life calm and without disruptions.

But he felt like a dried-up leaf. Maddie had brought the rain, but she'd also brought the sunshine. She had kicked the life back into him. She had made him aware of all he'd been missing the past years. She'd given him a taste of possibilities. She'd made him want, then satisfied him. She'd made him feel, and he almost resented her for that. Not feeling had been easier.

It was Wednesday night, and Joshua heard Benjamin Palmer buzz to a stop on his Harley. Patrick shot up from the kitchen table and walked to open the front door. "Wonder what she sent this time," he said.

"I don't know," Joshua muttered, and joined his son.

With eyes so like Maddie's, Ben shot Joshua a cocky, denigrating glance, then nodded at Patrick. "How ya doing, bud?"

"Pretty good. School will be out in a few weeks. I can't wait."

Brooding, Joshua watched the two as they conversed. He was fairly certain the only reason Ben hadn't added arsenic to the food was because of Patrick.

"She sent chicken stir-fry and rice. You'll probably need to heat it up. The brownies are awesome. I negotiated a batch in trade," Ben said, grinning slyly at Patrick.

"You're lucky," Patrick said. "You can eat Maddie's food anytime."

"Thank you for bringing the meal," Joshua told Ben. "I'd appreciate it if you'd tell Maddie I said thank you, too."

Ben looked at him as if he'd just as soon spit at him. "It's not gonna make a helluva big difference. You screwed up."

Joshua didn't blink. "Yeah, I did."

Ben's eyes widened briefly in surprise, then he turned back to chat with Patrick.

When he started to leave, Joshua gave in to a growing need to know what Maddie was doing. "How is she?"

Ben paused. "Fine," he said. "She's busy, but she

always worked at staying busy when something was bothering her. Right now an IRS auditor is trying to make sense of last year's return."

Joshua frowned. He was reasonably certain tax accounting wasn't Maddie's forte. "Has she got a tax accountant?"

"I don't think so. What do you care?" he asked belligerently. "All you wanted was a roll in the—"

He didn't get out the rest of his statement before something inside Joshua snapped and he shoved Ben against the wall. "I told you," he said, meeting the younger man's defiant gaze, "I screwed up. I'm paying for it. She's gone, and I wake up knowing it every single day."

Ben shrugged against the hold and stared at him. "Well, if you're that unhappy about it, and you're damn sure you're not going to hurt her again, then why don't you do something about it?"

"Everywhere But The Moon Tours," Maddie said into the phone, wishing she could go to the moon. "This is Maddie. How can I help you?"

After spending her lunch hour trying to reason with the IRS representative, she was convinced the man had ice water in his veins instead of blood. She was also convinced that one of the all-time great American lies was, "Hello, I'm with the IRS, and I'm here to help you."

Pushing aside her anxiety about her audit, she listened to the customer's request for airline tickets and punched out the information on her keyboard, then gave a quote.

"Which credit card—" She faltered when a cup of ice cream and a pink plastic spoon was placed on her desk in front of her. She slowly glanced up and saw a pair of hard muscular thighs encased in snug denim, a leather belt and gold buckle, a flat abdomen, well-developed chest and broad shoulders. She looked up a little farther and saw Joshua regarding her intently. Her heart slammed into overdrive.

The customer chanted the numbers to his credit card, but Maddie didn't take them down. She shook her head and looked away from Joshua. "I'm sorry. Could you repeat that, please?"

She had to shade her eyes to focus, but she managed to get the appropriate information and ring off. She looked at Joshua again and blinked to make sure she hadn't imagined him. Again.

"Hi," she said. She'd delayed seeing him because she'd known it would knock her sideways. She'd hoped time would soften the impact. It hadn't.

"Hi," he said, and his voice did the same scary, wonderful thing to her stomach.

She took a careful breath and tried not to stare. He looked so good, but was so bad for her. "Well, what are you doing here?"

He nodded toward the ice cream. "You never got to eat your ice cream that night we were together."

She glanced at it and fought a sensual, emotional tidal wave. The night they'd made love. She pushed her hair back from her face and produced a smile. "What a nice surprise," she murmured, and pulled off the top.

Whipped cream. A lump formed in her throat.

"Underneath the butterscotch syrup and sprinkles there is some ice cream," he said in a wry tone.

How was she going to eat this? All she could think of was the erotic taste of Joshua and whipped cream. Her mind was filled with the image of Joshua taking her, and her taking him.

Extremely conscious of his gaze on her, she forced a small bite in her mouth. "It's delicious."

"Good." He sat on the edge of her desk. "I wondered if you would go with me for ice cream on Friday."

She had wondered if he would come around again. She had hoped for it, feared it, avoided it. She'd even bribed Ben to deliver Joshua's meals so she wouldn't have to face him. Cowardly? Perhaps. Maddie preferred to view it as prudent. While she'd never been particularly prudent before, she thought it might be a good idea to develop the attribute.

So far it went against her grain. But she wasn't giving up yet. She had too much to lose.

Not only that, she was wearing three guardian angel pins under her collar to protect her from temptation. Temptation was sitting right in front her, and it wasn't the ice cream.

She cleared her throat. "I don't think that's a good idea."

He leaned closer. "Why not?"

He made the words sound intimate; his mouth was close, and she could see the wanting in his gaze. The same wanting she felt inside. It would be so easy to lift her lips for him to take.

His eyes could turn her to liquid, his voice dissolved her resolve. He was the best and worst kind of temptation. *Lead me not into temptation,* Maddie thought desperately. I have no problem getting there all by myself.

She sucked in a deep breath and backed away. "Because you have a bad habit of melting my—" *Everything,* she thought. You melt my everything. But she glanced down at her disintegrating dessert and said, "Ice cream."

On Saturday morning she had the stereo cranked up to concert level. If she had to revisit her tax return for the tenth time, then U2 could help her through it. She'd set Davey's swing to rock for twenty minutes, and every now and then she tickled his toes and made kiss noises on his feet. She was flipping through old receipts and canceled checks when someone banged on her front door.

She debated answering it. So far, one charity and two religious organizations had solicited her. Grudgingly, she rose and opened the door.

Joshua and a preppy-looking man stood on her porch.

Maddie's gaze latched on to Joshua, and she felt that familiar, cursed, sinking sensation. What was he doing here? After turning down his offer for ice cream and anything else he might have in mind, she'd assumed he wouldn't come for her anymore. After all, Joshua could have any number of women. That fact did nothing to elevate her mood.

Irritated that she was going to have to shoo him away again, Maddie thought about her guardian angels and frowned. She was doing her best to fight her desire for Joshua and she could use some help.

Joshua's mouth was moving, but she couldn't quite make out his words. "Pardon?" she said.

With a wry half grin, he shook his head and walked past her to turn down the volume of the stereo. "I understand you've been going a couple of rounds with the IRS, so I brought a friend who can help. This is Roger Hensley. He's my tax accountant."

Nonplussed, she hesitated, looking from Joshua to Roger. She extended her hand. "Thank you. It's very nice to meet you." She had no idea how to act toward Joshua. This went far beyond ice cream. It was thoughtful, considerate. She might almost believe she truly mattered to him. Her heart swelled in hope, and she scolded herself. She'd been fooled before.

"Maddie," Roger said, "do you mind letting me take a look at your return?"

Torn for only a second, she shook her head. "Not at all. I'd be very grate—" She broke off when Joshua caught her eye. The tension thrummed between them. There'd been gratitude and too much more, but she couldn't afford to turn down an offer of help at this stage. "I'd appreciate it," she said, then went to collect the forms.

Two hours later Roger had worked his accounting magic and straightened out her return. He gave her his business card as he left. "If the gladiator from the IRS has any questions, you can tell him to call me."

She offered to pay him, but he held up his hands

and assured her it was covered. After he was gone, she turned slowly to Joshua, who was holding Davey as he slept. The image tugged at her heart, reminding her of secret wishes and dreams, reminding her of her foolish hopefulness. She tried to block her feelings.

It was nearly impossible. "That was very nice," she told him. "Why did you do it?"

Joshua looked momentarily uncomfortable. "You needed help. It wasn't difficult to arrange."

Maddie nodded and took Davey from Joshua. "No big deal?" she asked in a quiet voice. "No big deal to get a tax accountant to make a house call on a Saturday morning."

He shrugged. "He's an old friend. A nice guy."

"What did you give him?" When he looked as if he was going to deny it, she cut him off at the pass. "And don't lie."

"Discount stud service for his mare." His eyes glinted with sexual innuendo. "Don't worry, Maddie. No one will suffer."

She groaned and walked away, taking Davey to his crib. Her mind was whirling. Why was he doing this? It made no sense. Joshua had made it clear he wanted her for a good time. She'd made it clear she needed more now. So why was he playing with her? Why was he doing things for her?

Returning to the den, she confronted him. "I appreciate your friend's help with my taxes very much, Joshua. But I don't understand why you came to see me at work the other day or today."

He walked toward her. "I've missed you."

Her stomach turned a somersault. "You have?" She heard the cracked surprise in her own voice and cleared her throat.

"Yeah." He lifted a strand of hair from her cheek. "Have you missed me?" he asked in a low voice.

Too much. She swallowed. "I—uh—I thought it would be best if we didn't see each other."

Joshua nodded and moved closer. "I disagree."

Maddie stepped backward, trying to create some desperately needed space between them. "We want different things. You want fun. I need— Ouch!" Her heel banged against the baseboard.

"You rushed me," he told her in a mild tone.

She looked at him in confusion. "I rushed you?"

"I'd just gotten started and you decided it was over."

Despite his closeness, she tried to keep a clear head. "I thought it was best—"

"Best for who?" he demanded, trailing his fingertips down her bare arm.

She ignored the tingling sensation. "Best for both of us."

"Not for me," he told her, and lowered his mouth to hers.

She ducked her head and dodged him, barely. Oh, Lord, she could practically taste him, she thought, closing her eyes for a second.

He took a different tack and brushed his lips over her bangs. "I've missed you. I want to know that you've missed me, too."

Her heart squeezed tight. She feared saying yes to him, feared it would precipitate a slew of other *yeses* she shouldn't even be thinking. "That doesn't really matter," she insisted. "We want different things."

"Go to lunch with me," he said, dropping his mouth to her neck.

Maddie shook her head. "No."

"Tell me you've missed me."

"No." She whispered the lie and bit back a groan when he pressed against her from chest to thigh. He was strong, and he felt so right. But it was so wrong. She pushed against him and squeezed underneath his arm, holding out her hand for him to stop when he walked toward her again.

"We're nowhere near finished yet," he told her, determination stamped on his face.

The power of his confidence could have daunted her if she didn't have a stubborn will of her own. She suspected, however, that she was going to need more than three metal angels from the card shop, if she was going to stand her ground.

She lifted her chin. "You're not calling all the shots, Joshua. It takes two, and I don't want to play with you anymore."

His gaze skimmed over her possessively. "Then I'll have to change that, won't I? And, sweetheart, here's fair warning, I've just gotten started."

He walked out the door, leaving Maddie to wonder when salt-of-the-earth, stick-in-the-mud Joshua had turned into the very devil.

Eleven

By the time Joshua got out of the barn, Maddie was roaring up his lane, away from the house, away from him. Her muffler buzzed like a giant mutant bee.

Even in the rain he could see the exhaust from her tailpipe. He threw his rake to the ground and swore. His best opportunity for catching her in days, and he'd missed her.

The volume of her motor abruptly increased, and he narrowed his eyes. He jogged farther up the lane and saw an object lying in the road. Despite his ill mood, he chuckled when he identified it. This evening might turn around for him yet.

Turning out of Joshua's driveway, Maddie floored her accelerator and frowned at how loud her engine sounded. She couldn't hear her radio. She couldn't hear herself think. She checked on Davey. He looked numb.

Maddie supposed some might say she'd acted like a chicken by running in and out of Joshua's house so quickly. But she would disagree. She was trying to be prudent again.

Chicken.

"Prudent," she retorted aloud, but was barely able to hear herself.

She continued down the road when a siren sounded. Glancing in her rearview mirror, she cringed and immediately glanced at her speedometer. She wasn't speeding. What could be wrong?

She pulled to a stop on the side of the road and waited, a sense of dread settling in her stomach. She'd never dealt well with authority figures.

The officer strolled alongside her car. He tipped his hat. "Ma'am, are you aware that it's illegal to operate a vehicle without a muffler?"

Nonplussed, she shook her head. "But I have a muffler. I know I do. I know—"

The officer smiled and shook his head. "No ma'am, you don't, and I'm gonna have to give you a ticket."

"But—"

A truck came to a stop beside her. Joshua's truck, Maddie realized. She didn't know whether to duck or be relieved.

Getting out, he pulled something long and rusty from the bed of his truck. "Looking for this?" he asked Maddie with a smart-aleck grin.

"How are you, Abel?" he said to the officer.

"Slow day when you pick on young mothers with babies, isn't it?"

Abel winced. "She's a mom? Damn, I didn't see a baby in there." He shoved his pad of tickets back into his pocket. "That her muffler?"

"Yep, she left it in my driveway."

"Okay, Josh. Make sure it gets fixed. Don't let me catch her without it again. Evening, ma'am," he said to Maddie, then strolled back to his car.

"Male chauvinist," she muttered under her breath, and met Joshua's gaze. "May I have my muffler, please?"

"Sure," he said, putting the rusted metal in her back seat. "But if another cop stops you, you'll probably get a ticket."

She brushed her hair back in frustration. "How am I supposed to get to a service station to get it fixed?"

He leaned against her window. "I know a guy who might be willing to fix it for you tonight."

Maddie was skeptical. "And charge me an arm and a leg?"

Joshua shook his head. "No more than you'll pay tomorrow in town."

"Lead on," Maddie said.

Joshua's lips tilted in a wicked grin. "You can join us for dinner."

Maddie's stomach flipped. Why did he make her feel like she was going to be dinner?

An hour later, after they'd finished the meal and Patrick had disappeared into his bedroom to do homework, Maddie put Davey down for a nap on a blanket. She'd been leery of leaving him there with

Major so close by, but the dog acted as if it was his job to watch the baby. He sat and watched, and after a few minutes, closed his eyes.

Joshua urged her outside on the front porch. "C'mon, you can see him through the door. It's stopped raining."

Weary of fighting him, Maddie threw in the towel for the evening. She wouldn't be staying much longer because her muffler would be fixed, and he hadn't jumped her during dinner.

She looked up at the winking stars in the sky and took a deep breath. "It really is beautiful, here. You don't have to contend with the lights from the city."

He came to stand behind her. "Yeah. It reminds me of that night we were together on the hill," he murmured.

Maddie's insides tightened in remembrance. Joshua had been tenderly persistent for her pleasure. He had held her as if he would never let go, made love to her as if she were the most important woman in the world to him. He'd made her giddy.

She felt his hand on her hair and held her breath.

"I've never wanted a woman like I want you, Maddie."

She swallowed past her tight throat. "It's been a long time for you," she said. "That's all."

He gave a dry chuckle. "It would be a helluva lot easier if that was all." He slid his hand around her waist and pulled her against him. "What would you think if I told you I hadn't dreamed in years?"

She knew she should move away, but his statement distracted her, surprised her. She looked up at him. "What?"

"What would you think if I told you I hadn't dreamed in years?"

Maddie shook her head. The idea was difficult to comprehend. "I can't imagine it. How can you not dream? You go to bed at night and you dream."

"Not me," he said, and sifted his fingers through her hair. "I didn't dream for years."

"But that changed?"

"Yeah." He continued to stroke her hair. His touch was both soothing and sensual, and she would stop him. In a minute.

"When did you dream again?"

"The first time?"

She nodded, and his fingers slid down her neck. Her insides dipped and swayed. It was easy and hard to be held by him. Easy because it felt so good and right. Hard because she knew better.

"The first time I had a dream was when you kissed me for changing your tire."

Maddie's heart stopped. "What?"

His gaze met hers and he continued to stroke downward. "I dreamed the night you kissed me."

"What did you dream?"

He wore an expression of mingled disgust and disbelief. "Buttercups."

She couldn't suppress a light laugh. "How did it feel to dream again?"

"I liked it, but I didn't dream again until you kissed me again."

A smidgen of doubt crept in. "That's odd," she said.

"No kidding," Joshua muttered. "I thought it was coincidence until it happened again. Strange as hell."

She was torn. He sounded as skeptical as she felt.

His gaze locked on hers, he slid his fingers underneath the top of her blouse to her breasts. "Oh, Maddie, you have no idea what you do to me." He lowered his mouth to hers and plucked at her nipple.

She should be saying no right now, she thought, but her mouth was opening to him, her tongue wrapping around his in an intimate caress. She should be pushing his hand away, but her breast was swollen and budding beneath his touch.

She felt like a meteor shower was falling inside her, and she didn't want it to stop. If she had superpowers, she could pull back right now, but Maddie had always been extremely human. Never more human than right now.

"Oh, Maddie, I want you," he murmured against her mouth. "I want you back."

In the back of her mind she heard a voice, *Fool me once, shame on you. Fool me twice, shame on me.* Her heart tightened, and her doubts tumbled through her.

"You've turned me upside down," Joshua said, kissing her neck, still fondling her breasts. "Making me dream, then making me stop when you cut me off."

"Cut you off?" she repeated, grasping for a shred of sanity. She was torn between fear and arousal.

"Oh, yeah. The first time we made love, I dreamed

the whole night through. When you dumped me, the dreams completely stopped.''

Maddie backed away and stared at Joshua. Her head was reeling. She felt as if she were on a seesaw, and she didn't know which way to go. To believe or not believe. He looked trustworthy. He sounded as if he was telling the truth. But she'd been fooled before.

''Are you telling me you haven't dreamed since we made love?'' she asked, watching him closely.

He shook his head slowly. ''A few quick, vague visions, but no real dreams. I haven't dreamed at all since we were together under the stars.''

Maddie simply couldn't believe she could have that kind of impact on a man, especially a man like Joshua.

''You don't look like you believe me,'' he said.

''I'm having a very difficult time,'' she confessed. ''Do you know what it sounds like?''

He leaned against the railing and crossed his arms over his chest. ''What?''

''The most original line for getting laid I've ever heard.''

''Well, if it isn't Mr. Sleaze,'' Jenna Jean Anderson said, looking down her slim nose at him.

Joshua swallowed a sigh. Not an auspicious beginning, he thought. He was getting nowhere fast with Maddie, and the thought of not having her in his future turned his stomach. ''I need your help,'' he said bluntly.

Her eyes widened slightly. ''Help? Why should I

help you? You hurt my friend. You," she said, point-ing her finger at him, "Mr. Studfarm Owner—"

"I screwed up," he said, finishing for her. "She's the best thing that ever happened to me, and I want her back." He met her doubtful gaze without flinch-ing. "I think underneath it all she might want me, too. Are you letting me in, or not?"

She hesitated a long moment, then opened the door wider. "If you make me regret this, I'll find a way to torture you the rest of your life."

"I don't doubt it," he muttered, but walked inside her house.

"Have a seat." She motioned toward the sofa. "I haven't talked to Maddie in a few days. What have you done so far?"

In no mood for sitting, he paced. "I took her ice cream at work, got a tax accountant to straighten out her IRS problems and got her out of a ticket when her muffler fell off her car."

Jenna made a noise of disgust. "Maui strikes again." Her face cleared. "I'm impressed with the tax accountant. Nice touch."

"Thanks. It didn't work."

"When you apologized," Jenna began, and she must have read his expression. She rolled her eyes. "Oh, no, you didn't apologize."

He threw out his hands. "What do I apologize for? All I did was tell her she was an incredible woman and how special she was because she didn't need marriage." He shook his head. "How was I sup-posed to know she was even thinking about anything permanent?"

Jenna sighed. "I need some wine. Do you want some wine?"

"No. I've already tried whiskey. It doesn't work."

Jenna disappeared into the kitchen and returned with a glass. She sank into an overstuffed chair. "Would you please sit down?"

Joshua reluctantly sat.

"Okay, let's take this from the top. First the apology. Even if you don't think you said anything wrong, you can apologize for hurting her feelings." She took a sip. "There's also the matter of how you feel about a permanent, committed relationship."

"I want Maddie in my life."

"For how long?" Jenna asked, regarding him carefully.

Joshua had dodged this question with himself. The idea of making a commitment, even in his mind, when Maddie would barely accept his phone calls made him itch. In most instances he preferred hedging his bets.

"That's something Maddie and I will have to figure out," he said.

She lifted her eyebrows and seemed to consider him yet again. "I'm going to tell you something about Maddie. She has never had a man court her. She might deny that she would want such a thing, but she wouldn't be telling the truth. She was hooked up with Clyde for a long time, but he never bothered to find out what she wanted."

Joshua's mind immediately whipped through the little hints Maddie had innocently given him in their various conversations. Remembering one in particular, he swore under his breath and shook his head.

"What's wrong?"

"I can't play a kazoo, let alone a guitar," Joshua growled.

Maddie sang along with Bryan White and fed Davey his first rice cereal. She couldn't tell if he liked it or not, since most of it was on his hands and face. Unfortunately he'd flung some of it on her. Good thing it was Sunday morning and no one would see her in her current state. She'd pulled her hair into a high ponytail and wore an ancient T-shirt and denim cutoffs.

Watching his eyes dance and his feet kick, she smiled. His vibrant personality was becoming more apparent with each passing day. Bright and curious, he was a happy baby, but he had a little stubborn streak. He didn't sleep too much. Maddie suspected he didn't want to miss anything.

Maddie loved it when he gurgled. She was certain he would be musically inclined. She could thank Clyde for that. And she thanked her lucky stars that she'd given birth to her son. He was the joy of her life, her reason for rising in the morning, and lately, for putting one foot in front of the other.

Her smile faded. That was an awful lot to put on a little baby, she thought. It wouldn't always be this way, Maddie told herself. She wouldn't always feel such sharp pain when her mind wandered to Joshua. Soon she wouldn't think of him twenty-three of twenty-four hours a day. She wouldn't remember the way he'd held her and the way he'd made her feel, as if she were important, even vital. She wouldn't think about the crazy dreams she'd had about him.

Soon, she told herself. Soon.

The doorbell rang, interrupting her thoughts. Casting a quick glance at the clock, she wondered if it was Ben coming over to bum breakfast. Then she quickly put the baby down in his crib before heading to the door.

She opened the door to Joshua. The mere sight of him was enough of a surprise, but *roses?* She looked at the flowers, at him, then back at the flowers. She had to fight the urge to ask "Who died?" They couldn't be for her, she tried to tell herself, but no other logical reason for them came to mind. Her heart thumped faster.

Joshua narrowed his eyes. "What do you have in your hair?"

Maddie lifted her hand and felt her son's breakfast. "Rice cereal."

He gave a mock-perplexed look. "New beauty treatment?"

She shook her head. "You're so clever. Why are you here?"

His expression grew more intent. "To see you."

Her stomach took a quick dip, and Maddie bit back an oath. "To see me," she said skeptically. "Wearing rice cereal."

"Surely you're not surprised," he said, and walked past her into her house. Uninvited. "I've enjoyed seeing you with other foods on you. As a matter of fact I can recall seeing you wearing nothing but..." His voice trailed off as he flicked his gaze over her.

Whipped cream. Maddie's stomach took another dip as she closed the door behind him. For all her attempts at denial and forgetting, she knew she would never forget the whipped cream.

"These are for you." He offered the flowers to her.

Feeling a rush of pleasure and discomfort, she held the roses and smelled them. The first time she'd ever received flowers from a man. She didn't exactly know how to respond. "They're lovely," she said. "And unexpected. What possessed you?"

"A token of my affection." He said it with a straight face.

Her heart squeezed tight. "Thank you. Let me put them in water." She wheeled into the kitchen with Joshua following after her.

"I need to apologize," he said to her back.

Maddie nearly dropped the glass vase. The water running full force, she turned around and stared at him. "Excuse me?"

"I need to apologize. I hurt you. I didn't intend to."

Simple, but achingly sincere, his words cut straight to her heart. She took a deep breath. "I never thought you intended to hurt me. I just misread you." She turned the water off and tried to collect herself. "I just realized we were headed in different directions."

He cocked his head to one side. "Do you really think that? That we're headed in different directions."

Maddie blinked. "Well, yes. I'm looking for something permanent. You aren't." She repeated the same words to herself three times.

"I think you may be wrong."

"No," she said immediately. "I'm not."

"I think we'd both like to find out what we want with each other." He stepped closer and cupped her jaw. "I think you still want to be with me."

Maddie closed her eyes and groaned. "When are you going to stop?"

He pulled her against him, and she felt his solid strength and arousal. Why did she feel as if she fit this man like a second skin? Why did her heart fight with her mind to get closer to him?

He ran his open mouth over her lips, tempting her, promising her. "I'm not stopping until I get you," he told her, softening the punch of his sensual threat with his kiss.

Maddie kissed him back, and their caresses quickly grew out of control. He slid one of his hands up her shorts and with his other hand, guided her to touch him intimately.

We shouldn't do this. She heard it in her head, but had she said it aloud?

His fingers stroked her wet core. He rubbed her sensitive bead of pleasure, and she felt swollen inside and out. Needy for him. "Joshua," she said, knowing she should call a halt.

"Don't make me stop. You feel so good," he murmured. "You can blame it all on me," he said, and sucked her bottom lip into his mouth. "I need to feel you come apart in my hands."

That was all it took. His words and voice affected her like he was naked and inside her. She splintered, shattered, peaked. He made her shudder from her very depths until she slumped against him.

"Oh, Maddie, you're incredible. You're so beautiful. You have no idea how beautiful. You have no idea what you do to me," he told her, holding her tight.

Maddie's knees still trembled. She felt torn in two. It was as if her body knew she belonged to him, but her mind refused to allow it. "Oh, Joshua, this is craziness," she said breathlessly, and was mortified at the tears threatening behind her eyes. She swallowed over a lump in her throat.

Squeezing her eyes shut, she ducked her head against his chest. His strength, his heartbeat and scent were so familiar they felt as if they were a part of her. "I don't want to fool myself again," she told him. "When I'm with you, I feel a little out of control." She shook her head and made herself look up at him. "That's scary. I don't want to feel stupid for believing things might work out when they won't."

He paused a long moment, his gray eyes shifting like storm clouds. "Everyone's got their own doubts to tangle with," he finally said. "There's only one solution." His voice was firm, almost hard. "You've got to meet me halfway."

Maddie's throat tightened, because she feared Joshua's concept of meeting halfway would be like trying to leap across the Grand Canyon.

Twelve

A few nights later Joshua sat on Maddie's hill. Yes, he owned the property, but some crazy part of him had decided Maddie owned the hill. He thought about his life, his heart, and wondered if she owned more than the hill.

Joshua hadn't spent the past twelve years searching his soul about why Patrick's mother had died. He'd been too busy building his business and too clueless about raising a son on his own to do a lot of soul searching.

Lately, however, Joshua had done an awful lot of thinking, and some of it hadn't been enjoyable. He wondered if, deep down, he had blamed himself for Gail's death. As a high school senior, he'd been the one to talk her into going all the way in his car. He'd been the one to forget about contraception.

She'd been the one to pay.

The unfairness upset him. Why'd she have to die? Why'd it have to go so terribly wrong? Why'd Patrick have to grow up without a mother?

The thoughts made his chest feel heavy with regret. He remembered walking around bearing this heaviness for years, but staying too busy to figure out the source of it. Now, he knew.

And the reason he knew was Maddie. She made the heaviness go away. She gave him hope. She made him feel the sunshine and taste the rain.

He craved her presence. She talked about being scared. He laughed without humor. If she knew how much he craved her, it would probably scare the living daylights out of her. It sure as hell disturbed him.

For so long it had been safe to stay uninvolved, to keep his heart and life locked away. It had been a relief not to dream or feel too much. Now, however, it was as if Maddie had shown him another world, and Joshua didn't want to leave. He smiled darkly to himself. No matter how hard she tried to push him away, he thought as he stared into the darkness, he wanted her.

A moment passed and he caught sight of Patrick walking toward him. From his seated position in the grass, Joshua was especially aware of Patrick's height. Where had the years gone? he wondered, but didn't voice the thought. Although Joshua hadn't met all his son's needs, he had the satisfaction of knowing he'd done his best, and Patrick had flourished. For his age he was a responsible, levelheaded kid. Worthy of his father's trust and respect.

When Joshua looked at Patrick, he thought maybe he hadn't screwed up too badly after all.

Patrick's gaze was curious. "You got a call from some Randolph woman. She says her mare's in season."

Joshua nodded. "She's early, but we can handle it."

Patrick shoved his hands in his pockets. "So, uh, what are you doin' up here?"

Joshua's lips tilted. He knew he was acting strange as hell. "Listening," he said. "Looking at the stars."

Patrick looked at him. "Oh." He looked up at the stars, then back to Joshua. "Does this have anything to do with Maddie?"

Joshua cocked his head to one side. His son had good instincts. "Yeah. I've been thinking about Maddie some lately."

"Are you gonna marry her?"

His neck muscles tightened and he rubbed the back of it. "I haven't decided."

"Do you love her?"

Joshua paused a half beat. He wasn't exactly happy with the truth yet. "Yeah, I think I do."

"Do you think she loves you?"

Joshua's heart softened. "Yeah, I think she does, son." He looked into Patrick's searching gaze. "It takes more than love, sometimes."

Patrick shrugged as if he didn't understand. "Well, if you decide to marry her, I like having her around."

Joshua swallowed a grin. "Are you sure? What about Davey? Babies make a lot of noise."

Patrick shook his head. "He's an okay baby. Not too cranky. And he only throws up a little bit."

"That's true, but Maddie's a woman, and when they move into a house, they like to change things."

Patrick's eyes narrowed in wariness. "What kind of things?"

Joshua thought back to his earlier life. "Oh, they put perfume and makeup bottles all over the bathroom, and they like to put knickknacks around the house. They get upset when you leave socks on the floor, and like you to clean your room on a regular basis."

Patrick was silent for a long moment. "Since you've got a master bath, she'd probably put the perfume in your bathroom. The knickknacks are no big deal, but we might have to talk about cleaning my room." He gave a wily grin. "Maybe for brownies."

Joshua laughed. "You've been taking lessons from Ben."

"Ben's cool," Patrick said. "Speaking of Ben, he-uh-let me drive his motorcycle."

Joshua raised his eyebrows. Patrick knew Joshua didn't like the idea of him driving a motorcycle yet. "He did?"

"Yeah. I was supercareful," he rushed to say. "I wore a helmet and didn't drive too fast or anything. I've got another computer class after school tomorrow, and I was hoping you would let me drive the motorcycle to school."

Joshua's automatic response was no, but then he saw the undiluted hope on his son's face. Patrick was a good kid. Worthy of trust. He took a deep breath.

"This won't be a regular occurrence," he said, "and—"

"Al-l-l-l-l-right!" Patrick yelled. "Dad, you won't regret this. I'll be so careful."

"You damn well better be." Joshua stood. "Wear the helmet."

"I will."

"And you drive defensively, because people don't see motorcycles as easily as they see cars."

"I know."

"Keep your distance and no showing off," Joshua continued. "Even if the girls are watching."

Patrick just grinned. "I won't."

Joshua made it inside his front door just as Maddie whirled from the kitchen. Her eyes flew open wide in surprise. She'd obviously finagled a key from Patrick, and the little scamp was trying to sneak away without seeing him.

"In a rush again?" he asked mildly, leaning against the door.

She straightened her posture. "Not a tremendous hurry," Maddie said. "I understand you've been busy with settling and breeding and studding and stuff...." She waved her hands. "So I didn't want to interrupt your schedule."

Why not? Joshua thought. You've interrupted everything else. He lifted an eyebrow. "Studding?"

"Well, whatever it is that you do, or your horses do. You said something about settling and studs, so—"

He chuckled. "Close enough."

"Has all of that been going well? The mares are cooperative and the studs are—" She shrugged.

"The studs are always ready," Joshua told her, thinking how much the animal kingdom mirrored human mating rituals. "We don't usually have much problem with the mares unless someone has messed up with the calculations and testing and they're not in season."

She nodded. "And how do you know if it—" She searched for the word. "Takes?"

"The stick turns blue," he said wryly.

"Oh." She twined her hands together. "I don't know much about horses. I rode a pony a couple of times when I was a kid."

Confused, Joshua studied her. It had looked as if she was trying to avoid him again, but she wasn't bolting for the door right now. "Would you like to ride?"

"The stud?"

"No," Joshua said flatly, immediately. "He's mean, ornery, and the only thing he's good for is f—" He broke off to find a gentler term. "Settling mares. I have a real sweet older mare who would give you a nice ride."

She tilted her head to one side and smiled. "Is this your way of saying you don't think I can handle a stud?"

Joshua felt his blood began to heat. He would almost think she was flirting with him. "I know you can't handle my stud. My horse. But that's not to say I wouldn't want you handling anything of mine."

Her gaze met his. "Is that an invitation?"

The look in her eyes made him want to howl like a wild animal. "Yes," he said. "What do you think of that?"

She moved closer, close enough to touch. "I'm... thinking." She lifted her lips to his, and Joshua felt his heart pound against his rib cage. She felt so warm, so soft, so alive, so good, he would swear he heard bells.

"The phone's ringing," Maddie managed to say when she pulled back slightly.

He sucked in a deep breath and swore. Hell, he was so aroused he could have taken her against the wall. He debated answering the phone, then remembered he was waiting on a call about another stud he wanted to buy. "Just a minute," he said firmly. "Don't go anywhere."

He jogged to the kitchen and idly noticed the table set for three. Perhaps Maddie hadn't intended to cut and run after all. He picked up the phone. "Blackwell," he said.

"Mr. Blackwell, are you Patrick Blackwell's father?" a woman asked.

"Yes," he said, frowning a little. He never got calls about Patrick.

"I'm calling from Roanoke Memorial Hospital, and your son has been in a serious automobile accident. He has arrived in the emergency room and is being examined for treatment. May we have phone permission to treat your child?"

His blood turned to ice. "Patrick?"

"Yes, sir. May we have phone permission to treat your child?"

"How serious?"

"I'm not certain. He is being evaluated. May we have phone permission to treat your child?"

"How bad is it?"

"I'm sorry, Mr. Blackwell, but I'm not certain. He is being evaluated right now. May we have phone permission to treat your child so we can begin X rays and lab work?"

"Yes," he said, frustrated when he realized she wasn't going to disclose further information. He felt Maddie's gaze on him. "Tell him I'll be there as soon as I can." He placed the phone into the cradle, fighting a terrible, terrible fear.

"What is it?" Maddie asked.

He shook his head. "It was that motorcycle," he muttered to himself as he headed for the door. "That damn motorcycle. I knew I shouldn't have let him drive it. I should have gotten rid of it. It's pure temptation for a teenage boy."

He felt her take his arm. "Joshua, what happened?" she demanded.

"It's Patrick. He's in the emergency room. I've gotta go."

"Oh, no." She paused barely a heartbeat. "Well, I'm going, too."

His mind moving a mile a minute, Joshua shook his head. "I don't know how long this will take. Don't know his condition. She mentioned X-rays. That means he's probably broken something. A motorcycle accident can be messy," he said, and felt a slice of pain at the scenarios running through his head.

Grabbing her purse, she looked at him incredulously. "I'm coming with you."

Something inside him resisted the idea, although he couldn't say why. His mind was on Patrick. "What about Davey?"

"I'll call Jenna Jean or Ben from the hospital. Do you want me to drive?"

She was serious, he thought, as they both ran to his truck. He almost laughed, but thoughts of Patrick prevented him. "I don't have time to stop for a trooper if you get a ticket."

Maddie sighed. "Good point."

During the drive, in some corner of his mind, he noticed the way Maddie tried to reassure him. She touched his arm, asked a few questions that required one-word answers and said, "I think he'll be okay."

Joshua wondered and worried. Something inside him wouldn't allow him to accept her comfort. He'd had too much practice handling tragedy alone. After he checked emergency registration, a nurse's aide led him into a separate room. His throat tightened with each passing second until the doctor arrived.

"Concussion," the doctor said. "His leg is broken in two places, and he needs sutures. According to the police, the accident wasn't his fault. He tried to avoid it."

Joshua's gut twisted viciously, and he stiffened. He shouldn't have allowed Patrick to drive the motorcycle. "Is he conscious?"

"For the most part," the doctor said. "He's still a little confused. He keeps telling the nurses he tried to get out of the way."

"He's such a good kid," Maddie said, and gently squeezed his arm. Comfort, he thought, and was almost lulled into turning to her. But Joshua turned away instead. He couldn't accept comfort while his son was in pain.

"Yeah, he is," Joshua said. "I want to see him."

"He hasn't been cleaned up," the doctor said.

"I want to see him." He looked at Maddie. "If you need to go home…"

Maddie shook her head. "I'll wait. Can you let me know how he is?"

"Yeah." He nodded as he moved away. It was peculiar as hell, but he felt a sense of loss as soon as he'd taken three steps. The feeling confused him, but he didn't have time to think about it. "I'll let you know as soon as I can."

Joshua knew it was every parent's nightmare to see their child bleeding and in pain in the emergency room. When he saw Patrick, however, he felt as if his heart was ripped out of his chest. He had to grit his teeth together to block his emotions.

Patrick looked up at him like he was drowning. "Dad. I swear it wasn't my fault. I tried to—"

Joshua shook his head and squeezed Patrick's shoulder. "Hush. I know you did your best. Let's concentrate on getting you taken care of."

He didn't stray from Patrick's side through the stitches or when they set his leg. He sent a nurse out to tell Maddie the status, but it was hours before Patrick was taken to a room.

With his son asleep, Joshua walked into the waiting room to grab some coffee. He was surprised to find Maddie still there.

She rose to her feet as soon as she saw him. "How is he?"

He rolled his shoulders. "He's gonna be okay. That broken leg won't be a cakewalk, but he's gonna be okay."

Maddie sensed the easing of tension in Joshua. "What can I do for you? Is there something you need done at your house, or can I get you some food, or—"

He shook his head. "Nothing. I'm okay. I made a call to one of the men who works for me, and he'll cover everything. You should go home. You shouldn't have spent the night in the waiting room."

Feeling superfluous, she studied him. He seemed distant to her. "You've had a long night," she said softly.

He shrugged. "I've had a lot of practice getting through long nights."

But you didn't have to go it alone, this time. She brushed the thought away, but it persisted. "Are you sure I can't do anything?"

"Let me give you a ride home."

She shook her head. "No, Ben kept Davey for me. He called a couple of times asking about Patrick, and he told me he would come and get me."

He raked a hand through his hair. "Are you sure?"

"Sure," she said, reaching her arms around him, but he felt stiff and remote. "You can relax," she whispered. "A hug isn't supposed to hurt."

He gave her a quick squeeze, then backed away, and his gaze seemed to go right through her.

"I'll check on you later," she said.

He gave a noncommittal nod and walked down the hall.

Maddie watched him, relieved that Patrick would be okay, but concerned about Joshua. His distant response troubled her.

She phoned Ben, and he took her home. During the drive, after she filled him in on Patrick, she brooded over Joshua's behavior.

"Mad, you're making me nervous. You haven't been this quiet since you found out you were pregnant." Ben paused and grimaced. "You're not pregnant again, are you?"

She rolled her eyes. "No. I'm not pregnant. I was thinking about Joshua and how aloof he seemed last night and today." She frowned in concentration. "I know he was very worried about Patrick, but he seemed to close in on himself."

"Joshua is a major league loner. He's used to coping on his own."

She glanced at Ben. "I agree, but what makes you say that? He hasn't allowed women into his life for several years, but he's always had Patrick."

"All the more reason for him to stand alone. He's probably so used to putting out fires on his own, he doesn't know what to do with another human, let alone a woman."

Maddie could argue the issue of whether or not Joshua knew what to do with a woman, but perhaps Ben had a point. "You're saying he's dealt with crises on his own so much, that he doesn't know how to share them."

Ben nodded as he pulled into her driveway. "Yep," he said. "And I bet Joshua's not the type to ever learn."

The thought didn't comfort Maddie. Since he had told her to meet him halfway, Maddie had taken another turn and opened herself to him again. She scowled at herself. Who was she fooling? When had she successfully shut him out?

But now she needed to take a hard look at his behavior. What if he shut her out? She already knew he would stand by her during a crisis of hers. But would she be able to accept him keeping her at arm's length during his rough moments?

She shook her head. Even with all the changes she'd been through in the past year, Maddie knew she was not a woman for half measures. Although she might be more careful now, she would never be prudent. She had a go-for-it quality, and it had been responsible for her triumphs and losses.

She wondered, when all was said and done, which way it would end with Joshua.

Thirteen

Joshua pulled his front door shut behind him and leaned against it. Not bothering to turn on a light, he just stood in the silent darkness and sighed. The doctor said he wanted to keep Patrick for observation one more night. Everyone, including Patrick, had told Joshua to go home.

So, here he was, forced to face the absence of the noisiness and frantic pace of the hospital. At the hospital there were a hundred interruptions. Take the blood pressure, check his sutures, take his temperature, give him lunch... On and on it went. The routine had offered little peace, but it at least had kept the demons at bay.

It had kept him from wondering if he'd failed Patrick by allowing him to ride the motorcycle. It had kept him from memories of Gail's repeated stays at the hospital, and that last trip to the emergency room when nothing could be done. It had almost kept him from missing Maddie.

"Another long day," a soft feminine voice murmured from the other side of the room. "No rest for the wicked."

Joshua's eyes flew open. It was Maddie. He couldn't distinguish much more than the shape of her because of the darkness of the room. "Where are you?"

"Coming closer," she said, walking toward him. She pressed a glass into his hand and he breathed in her scent. "Drink up. How's Patrick?"

He automatically swallowed the wine. It was cool and pleasantly dry. "Patrick will be okay. The good news is the motorcycle was totaled," he said. "So the temptation will be removed."

"Maybe," she said. "Have you had dinner?"

He concentrated. "I think. Yeah, I had a couple of burgers." Watching her eyes glint in the darkness, he took a few more gulps and the wine was gone. "What are you doing here?"

"Checking on you." She took the glass. "Let me get you more wine."

"I'll turn on the light," he said.

"No," she said immediately. "Take a seat on the sofa and relax."

Why? he thought about asking, but his weariness won and he slumped onto the sofa. He watched Maddie return and accepted the refilled wineglass as she sat beside him.

"On a scale of one to ten, how terrified were you when you got the call yesterday?" she ventured.

Still tense, Joshua rolled his shoulders. "Twenty."

"And when Joshua Blackwell handles a crisis, he does it alone."

He met her gaze. "It's the only way I know."

"No hugs, no comfort, no sharing," she continued, sliding closer to him.

He inhaled deeply, still waiting for the tight feeling in his chest to loosen. "I can't remember having any of that."

She put her hand on his arm and rubbed her mouth on his cheek. "Then maybe it's time for you to make some new memories."

She took his wineglass and reached across him to set it on the end table. She felt warm and smelled of a sweet, alluring perfume. "Maybe it's time for you to learn a new way," she said, and kissed him.

His chest finally expanded, but other parts of his body tightened. Her mouth was sweet and ardent, her hands both soothing and seductive. He breathed deeply, wanting to inhale her, absorb her. Then, he sensed, all would be right. It wasn't that he couldn't survive without her, he told himself. It was that he didn't want to be without her.

He felt her fingers unfasten the buttons of his shirt. "What are you doing to me, Maddie?"

Her lips lifted in a she-cat smile. "It's a surprise."

His gut twisted, and his pulse pounded in all his pleasure points. Before he could say anything else, she slid her hand over his chest and gave him a French kiss that sent his body temperature soaring.

He thought about asking his question again, but what she was doing felt so damn good, he decided to hang on for the ride. She was moving more than his body. Joshua had never felt so cherished and turned on at the same time. He hadn't known it was possible.

She lowered her mouth to his chest and her hand to his belt. As she skimmed her lips down his chest to his belly, he swelled beneath the very suggestion of her touch. In achingly slow movements, she unfastened his belt and lowered his zipper.

When her hand slipped beneath his briefs to his hardness, he groaned. "Oh, Maddie," he muttered.

She swirled her tongue around his belly button, then dipped it inside, and he groaned again. Her mouth was so warm and sweet he didn't want her to stop.

Draped across his thighs, she stroked him intimately with her fingers, cupping him. He was hard, throbbing, ready to climb the walls from her teasing touch.

She lowered her mouth still farther and paused. Joshua held his breath. Would she? A second passed and she took him into her mouth.

"Ah, Maddie." Joshua clenched his eyes shut at the incredible pleasure. He felt the flick of her tongue over his swollen masculinity and began to swear under his breath.

He gradually opened his eyes, and the sight of her with her lips caressing him intimately nearly sent him over the edge. Her hair whispered over his thighs and abdomen, and her hands stroked his skin. It was too erotic for words, but Maddie was doing more than making love to him, she was laying claim to his heart and mind.

His resistance and doubt slid from his grip. She was tenderly taking him past the point of return. Perspiration beaded on the back of his neck. He wove his fingers through her hair as she pushed him further and further.

He could barely breathe, and his entire body trembled from intense arousal. His heart was too full, the pleasure too much. Calling her name, he burst over the edge, falling, falling, until she caught him.

Taking deep breaths, he drew her tightly against him. Every other breath, he swore, or said her name. She kissed his neck and cheek.

Finally he collected himself enough to see straight, although he wouldn't have put money on being able to walk. He stared at her in the darkness. "You are incredible. Hell, what—" He shook his head and released a long breath. "What was that for?"

She curled against him. "There are lots of different ways to handle a crisis. You're used to doing it one way, all alone. I wanted to show you another way." Lifting her head, she brushed her hand against his hair. "There are lots of ways to be together in a crisis when you're with someone you love."

His heart swelled again in his chest and he kissed her. He wondered when he'd been more loved. He wondered when someone had given to him so unselfishly.

"I love you," she whispered. "You need to know that." Her eyes darkened with emotion and she took a breath. "You need to know something else, too. I'm not a fifty-fifty kind of woman," she said, her voice stronger as she sat away from him. "Not the halfway kind, either. When it comes to love, I don't do fractions. I give all of me." Her gaze boldly met his. "And I want all of you."

He watched in amazement as she stood. "Deal with it, Joshua. I love you."

Still reeling from her lovemaking and her words, he watched her walk out the door. *Out the door?* Who did this woman think she was? He pulled himself together and rose none-too-steadily to his feet. His damn knees were still weak, but he ran to the porch and caught her as she rounded the side of his house to where she must have hidden her car.

"Where in hell do you think you're going?" he demanded.

She gave him a double take. "Home. I thought you might need a little rest."

"After you rendered me nearly unable to walk?"

She blinked. "Are you complaining?"

"About you leaving, I am."

She paused. "Oh," she said, searching his gaze. "Well, reality bites. I don't have an overnight baby-sitter tonight, so I need to go home."

He took a deep breath and pulled her against him. "Maddie, you can't make love to me like that and just walk out."

"I thought women had more of a problem with that than men."

He shrugged. "I don't know about that. All I know

is I want you to stay." He swallowed. "I want you to stay forever."

Amazement shining in her eyes, she looked up at him. "Forever?"

He twined his fingers through hers. "I want to put a ring on your finger and make promises that I will keep. I love you, Maddie, and I want to love you for the rest of my life."

Then Maddie started crying and got his shirt wet, but Joshua didn't mind because he knew it was right. He would never spend a night without dreams or Maddie again.

Two months later they were married on her hill. It rained a little, but the sun came out and Maddie felt like that was pretty much what had happened throughout her life. It often rained, but the sun eventually came out. With Joshua, she finally felt as if she'd found a place where she fit. A place designed for her.

Her heart was too full to contain it all, and he gently teased her as she struggled with her tears. But it was an incredible day. Her two best friends in the world were beside her. Her brother and Patrick, who was healing quickly, stood by Joshua. The surprise that tipped it over the edge for her, though, was her father escorting her to the outdoor altar and her mother's appearance.

Without her knowledge, Joshua had visited her parents and helped them to see her in a different light. Now Davey would know his grandparents.

She made the vows and felt each one in her heart. When Joshua repeated his, she could see in his honest gray eyes that he would always love her. The wonder of it still took her breath.

He held her tight and kissed her. Then, after pictures, they led the caravan to a lovely small inn for the reception.

"Did you mind the rain?" she asked him.

Joshua shook his head and grinned at her. "No, I've gotten so I kinda like the rain."

"It wrecked my hair," she grumbled. "And I ripped the bottom of my dress when I got out of the car."

He kissed her on the nose. "You look beautiful."

"You look spotless," she accused.

"Time to cut the cake," Ben said, with Patrick by his side. "Save the mushy stuff for later and feed us now."

"It's always your stomach. You're so primitive," Maddie said.

He shrugged. "It makes me easy to bribe."

"He's got a point," Joshua said, walking with her to the table that displayed the three-tier devil's food cake with chocolate icing.

Maddie sliced two pieces and smiled for the camera. Then, in keeping with tradition, Joshua served her a bite from his hand. She licked his fingers and grinned at his surprise.

She took her turn and lifted the piece to his mouth. "Maddie," the photographer called. "Look this way."

She swiveled her head, and her hand swerved. She heard a collective gasp and jerked back around.

She'd rubbed the devil's food cake against Joshua's crisp, perfectly white tuxedo shirt.

"Oops." She winced at him. "Is this when I say you looked a little too perfect, anyway?"

He glanced down at his shirt and chuckled. "I thought you would at least wait until we got to our suite before you started eating things off me."

Maddie threw him a look of mock censure. "You have a dirty mind."

His gaze grew sensual and he drew her closer. "I learned from the best." The applause from the wedding guests faded from her consciousness as Joshua kissed her.

Later that night, after the toasts had been made and the rice had been thrown, Maddie sprayed herself with perfume and pulled on the negligee her friend Emily had given her. She glanced down at the golden band and diamond ring on her third finger. When he'd given her the diamond, Joshua had told her it was a star he'd pulled from the sky. She'd cried.

Now she was married. To Joshua.

Her heart squeezed tight, and she took a deep breath. She wanted tonight to be special. Jenna Jean was taking care of Davey, so Maddie could focus her undivided attention on her husband. She would tell him again how wonderful he was, and how much she loved him. Then she would show him.

She glanced in the mirror and saw a happy, happy woman. She hoped she could help make him just as happy. Opening the door, she walked out of the bathroom into the lushly decorated suite. The only light came from the bathroom. Joshua had turned out the rest of them. She curled her toes into the plush carpet and turned to find him on the bed.

She dropped her jaw at the sight of him. He was wearing nothing but a guitar. "Well, hello," she said, walking toward him. "What is this all about?"

He looked amused, but resigned. "You once told me you always were a sucker for a guy and a guitar."

She smiled. "So you bought a guitar?"

"I felt like I had to. And I learned a song."

Amazed, she put her hand to her chest and felt her eyes swell with tears. "For me? You learned a song for me."

Joshua held up his hand. "Don't get too excited. It's just one song. One very simple song."

"Play it! Play it!"

"Okay," he said, and placed his fingers on the strings. With intense concentration he started to play, and despite the fact that it wasn't an electric guitar, Maddie could clearly make out the well-known three-chord melody of "Louie, Louie."

She laughed and cried and threw her arms around him. Maddie Palmer Blackwell had gotten caught again. This time for good.

* * * * *

If you liked THE TROUBLEMAKER BRIDE, don't miss THE YOU-CAN'T-MAKE-ME BRIDE, the third book in Leanne Banks's exciting series, HOW TO CATCH A PRINCESS. *Coming this July.*